OVERDOSE

AN ER PSYCHOLOGICAL THRILLER

RADA JONES MD

APOLODOR

APOLODOR PUBLISHING

Print ISBN: 978-1-790-13921-7

Printed in the United States of America

DEDICATION

This book is dedicated to my ER folks.

You muddle your way through shifts seeing patient after patient on a full bladder, fueled by hope, adrenaline and stale coffee. You get cursed and bit and spat on. You laugh at things normal people wouldn't, just to keep from crying.

Together we saved patients, we lost patients, and we wondered what happened to those we lost sight of. Like soldiers, we stood together fighting death.

You are my people.

OVERDOSE

PROLOGUE

Twenty-four-year-old Eric Weiss wasn't planning to die. He wasn't even looking to get high. He was just trying to sleep.

He died anyhow.

1

DR. EMMA STEELE WAS LATE. Only twenty minutes to the start of her shift. She pushed the pedal to the metal.

She could make it past the old sedan. *I can't stop. I've got only five more minutes to get there and save lives.*

She stopped anyhow.

She knocked at the window, shivering in her faded scrubs.

"Can I help?"

An old lady. Crying.

"I'm stuck."

"Start when I tell you. Go really slow."

She shoved her floor mat under the spinning wheel.

"Go now!"

She pushed. The crocs slid back.

Darn. Where's a man when you need one?

She took off her crocs and pushed again.

The car crawled forward, then accelerated, spitting snow in her face. *Gone.*

Emma shook off the snow and sloshed to her car in her red socks.

I'm frozen. I'm late. Ann's going to bitch again. Twelve hours to go.

Stupid.

She'd barely made it through the doors when the shit storm started.

"Code 99, Room 3, Emergency Department," roared the overhead speakers.

The scrubs streamed toward Room 3.

Wailing sirens pierced the air, then choked. The flashing lights went dark as the ambulance pulled in.

Emma hit the silver-plated door opener with the back of her fist and walked sideways into the sharp cold outside. Suzy, the EMT, glanced at her as she opened the ambulance door. Her dark-chocolate skin shone with sweat. *Good, deep chest compressions*, Emma thought. Their eyes met. Suzy's shoulders softened, but she continued compressions. Joe, her partner, unlocked the stretcher. They slid it off the ambulance with a bump and headed to Room 3. Suzy kept on the chest compressions while giving report.

"Found down... no known downtime... roommate started CPR... we arrived nine minutes later... no pulse, agonal breathing... couldn't establish an IV... got an IO in the left tibia... gave epi x 3..." Her voice came in bursts as she continued pushing down on the breathless chest while walking sideways.

The air smelled like sweat and dread. Joe kept bagging, but little air went in. *He's bagging too fast, and the mask seal is bad.*

"How long have you been doing CPR?"

"Nineteen minutes. We gave Narcan IO, 2 mg, with no result."

"Where was he?"

"In his bedroom downtown. In his bed."

"Any history?"

"No."

"Anything at the scene?"

"An empty bottle of Scotch. A pill bottle in somebody else's name. The other rig has it."

"How old is he?"

"Twenty-four."

"We have an ID?"

"Eric. Eric Weiss."

"Did you ever get a pulse?"

"No."

He looked asleep. There was no livor mortis, the dark patches of death, on his skin. Emma touched his neck, feeling for a pulse. None. His blond hair, darkened by sweat, covered his eyes. She brushed it away softly with her gloved hand. She gently parted his eyelid between her fingers. The iris was glazed, the black pupil a tiny peppercorn. *Opiates.*

"We're going to take care of you, Eric," she promised, though she knew he couldn't hear. It didn't matter. She said it for the team as much as she said it for him.

"Narcan, 2 mg." *Heroin, morphine, oxycodone, even methadone—all opioids relieve pain. They also give users a high. That's what gets them addicted. Enough opioid will put them to sleep. More than that will stop their breathing and kill them. Narcan is the only antidote that can reverse opioids. If that's what this is.*

"IV access?"

"Working on it," Judy said, without looking up. She knelt near his right elbow. *She's a whiz with IVs. If she can't get it in, nobody can.*

"IO drill." Brenda went after it.

The kid lay on the ER stretcher, his chest rising and falling about two inches with every compression. Suzy stood back at the end of the line waiting for her turn to perform CPR again. She had delivered him, but she couldn't leave him. Still no blood pressure. For the lack of a heartbeat, the shattered line of the EKG danced with the rhythm of the compressions. Tom, the RT, respiratory therapist, took over the airway. His left hand pulled the livid face into the mask while his right squeezed the airbag. The escaping air made obnoxious farting sounds. *Poor mask seal.*

"How's he bagging?" Emma asked.

"Not great."

"Epi, then bicarb, then another 2 of Narcan." Emma looked at Sal, the ER pharmacist. "Let's get ready to intubate."

"What do you want for intubation?"

"Sux maybe, no sedation. He's out already."

"Succinylcholine," he confirmed. "How much?"

Emma looked the kid up and down. Skinny and not too tall. Seventy kilos maybe? "One hundred twenty."

"Epi given."

Emma moved to the head of the bed to assess the airway. *The neck is mobile and slender. No scars. Good strong chin— three fingers to Adam's apple. I should have enough room to get the tongue out of the way to expose the airway.* She lubricated, then loaded the metal stylet curved as a question mark into the soft plastic ET tube. She checked the suction. The oxygen saturation didn't read at all. *It doesn't matter now, does it? He doesn't bag well. He needs an airway. Simple as that.*

"Second 2 mg of Narcan given."

"Prepare a third, and one more of epi in 5."

"That's 6 of Narcan, yes?" Sal asked. Two mg of Narcan was a full dose. Six was a lot.

"It won't hurt him any," she said. Narcan didn't do much

to the body, except for throwing it into acute withdrawal. "Better in withdrawal than dead."

Sal nodded.

"I'm ready," Emma said.

She lifted the blade of the video laryngoscope and held it gently in her left hand with the tips of her fingers. The RT removed the mask covering the mouth. Emma pried the kid's teeth open with her right hand, then slid the plastic blade around the tongue until the blade tip came into full view on the screen. Secretions, a mass of white foam, blocked her view of the airway. *Opiates, of course, probably pulmonary edema. That's why he wouldn't bag.* She slid the blade forward another half-inch, then lifted the tongue with it until the epiglottis, the pink stalactite of tissue protecting the airway, fell into full view in the middle upper part of the screen, where it belonged. *Textbook, but for the damn secretions*, she thought, her eyes glued to the airway.

"Suction."

The RT slapped the Yankauer, the plastic cylinder attached to the suction tube in her right hand. She slid it through the open mouth, suctioning secretions and moving the tongue away to uncover the vocal cords. She removed the Yankauer and placed it on the stretcher, under the kid's shoulder, to free up her right hand.

"Tube."

The tube landed in her open right hand. She slid it in past the tongue and the blade. She looked inside the mouth until the tip went out of view, and then returned her gaze to the video screen.

"Hold CPR and check for a pulse."

She slid the tube further in, aiming for the white triangle between the vocal cords, the gateway to the trachea, the windpipe. The slanted tip of the tube got caught in one of the arytenoids, the curly little cartilages sheltering the cords. She pulled it back a quarter of an inch and then pushed it forward, only to have it catch again. *We're running out of time.* She pulled the tube out once more and gently twisted it left less than a quarter turn, then pushed it forward again. This time it appeared just between the arytenoids. Another half-inch forward and the tube slid into the trachea, where it belonged.

"Stylet."

The RT pulled out the rigid stylet. That allowed the soft ET tube to take the sharp turn into the airway. Emma pushed it in until the balloon went out of sight.

"Balloon."

The RT pushed in the air from the 10 cc syringe attached to the balloon. The balloon filled with air and sealed the airway. The RT secured the tube. The airway was safe.

"Restart CPR."

"Bilateral lung sounds. Nothing over the stomach."

"Oxygen sat?"

"Can't get it. No waveform."

"No pulse."

"We have a twenty in the right AC," Judy said.

"One more dose of Narcan. Then bicarb."

The RT took over the tube. "Twenty-four at the lip," he said, and the nurse recorder wrote it down.

"Fourth dose of Narcan in."

The RT suctioned the bloody foam inside the tube. Then again.

More CPR. Each tired provider took his place at the back of the line to rest and start over.

"Bicarb given."

"How long have we been doing this?" Emma asked.

"Thirty-four minutes," the recorder answered.

"So we have unknown downtime, then bystander CPR for ten minutes, then EMT CPR, and Narcan x 1 and epi x 3 via IO, then CPR x 34 minutes and Narcan x 3 and epi x 2.

"And bicarb x 1," Sal said.

"Let's give one more. And one more of Narcan."

"That's 10 mg of Narcan altogether."

"Yes." Emma looked at the dead body on the stretcher. *He's somebody's son. Somebody's lover. Somebody's life will never be the same again after today.* "How's he bagging?"

"Better," the RT said.

"Narcan 2 mg dose 5 given."

Emma looked at her team. "Anybody have any more ideas?" *They need to have a chance to air out any issues before it's too late. This one's going to be hard for all of us.*

Silence. They had done all they could.

The beeps of the monitors and the whoosh of air flowing in and out of the bony chest made the silence feel even more deadly.

"If there are no more ideas..."

ITSY BITSY SPIDER

I gots the shakes. Bad.
I need a fix.
"Look in the ambulance bay," he said.
I look.
I find it. A red bag with a skull on it.
I open it. It's my fix.
A foot-long brown paper parcel, slim. Heavy.
A picture. Car number on the back.
"That's the ticket to your next fix," he said.
"How do I tell you I'm done?"
He laughs.
That laugh.
It gives me goose bumps.
"I'll know."
I shiver.
I go looking for the car.

2
_____

EMMA LOOKED around the room one more time.

"If there are no more ideas…"

"The CO_2 is up!" The RT's voice, high-pitched with excitement, shattered the silence.

It's up indeed. Up to 35. The first sign of success. Pulse, maybe?

"Stop CPR."

In the silence of the room, the monitor held the beat like a metronome—125 beats/minute, his own. The heart was back.

"Blood pressure?

"Checking."

"Start an epi drip. Whatever pressure we have, it's going to fall as soon as the epi wears off. Let's get a Narcan drip. Get me the intensivist."

"You want an EKG?"

"Yes, please."

The heart is back. But after so long without a pulse, is the brain dead? She looked into the frozen blue eyes. The pupils were still pinpoints. *At least they're not fixed and dilated. He's got a chance. We did the best we could.*

The pressure was good. The pulse was holding.

"Oxygen sat 100 percent."

"Let's go down on the oxygen. Chest X-ray, please, OG tube, Foley. The whole nine yards. You all know the drill." She looked each of them in the eye. "Good job, team. You did well."

They smiled at her. "You too, Dr. Steele."

She smiled back.

With a well-practiced move, she took off her soiled gloves and dropped them in the trash. *No bad news today.* Speaking to the family was harder than running the code, especially if the patient was young, or even worse, a child. *It's hard even when they're one hundred years old and demented. They're all somebody's—mother, wife, child. Emotions run deep —grief, despair, guilt. Facing them is hard. It's easier to channel them into anger and lash out at the ER staff.*

"You know him?" Brenda asked.

"No."

"He's Joey's grandson. He's a nurse in the ICU."

Emma shuddered. That was awful news. Joey, their elderly clerk, had retired last year. He was an old friend and a good man. The kid being one of their own nurses didn't help either. Emma hoped she was wrong. *Maybe it's not an overdose,* she thought, but she knew better.

She went to the bathroom to steal a private moment. She washed her hands and face in cold water, rinsing away the sweat and the sting in her eyes. She looked in the mirror at the tired woman looking back. *Pale as a ghost.* She took her lipstick from her coat pocket and put on some, trying to look less dead.

I may not look any better, but I feel better. It's like donning a shield. They don't need to know how weary I am. She straightened her back, took a deep breath, and went back to work.

3

BACK AT HER DESK, Emma logged on to check the board. Nobody new, just the same headache in Room 11 and the fever in Room 5. She checked her iPhone. *Nothing from Taylor. Should have been home hours ago. She must be in another funk.* She texted another question mark.

Her neck ached. She rubbed it hard, her fingers digging into the achy knot just right of her spine. *I wish I could cut it out.* She grabbed her stethoscope and threw it over her right shoulder, heading to the headache in 11. Room 11 was one of the few double rooms they had left. Her colleague, Dr. Crump, Kurt to his friends of which she was no longer one, was already there. He was overdressed, as usual, in a well-cut suit and silk tie. He looked polished and expensive as he talked to the other patient in the double room, a heavy young woman with stringy purple hair falling over her tattoos. He sat on the corner of her bed. *He really shouldn't be doing that, not in this climate of sexual aggression and hyper-alertness to anything looking like it. Not with this patient. Her looks scream borderline personality disorder. They're as reliable as ticking bombs.*

His voice was soothing and low as he touched her hand. Emma considered letting him have the room to finish. She could go see the fever in Room 5 instead, rather than interfere with his patient encounter. The headache was texting and eating chips. She'd be fine for a few more minutes.

Kurt looked up. Their eyes met. His softness vanished. His left masseter, the little muscle at the bottom of his clenched jaw, twitched. *He's still angry. After all this time, he's still angry.*

They got along well in the beginning. He helped her learn the ropes. He'd taught her who to trust and who not to, where to go when she needed things done, and who to avoid. He'd been invaluable to her in her first weeks after residency. This rural ED in the middle of nowhere was nothing like the trauma center she'd trained at. Here, resources were scarce. She had to learn to do without. Specialties that she'd taken for granted were not available. The best way to care for the sickest patients was to transfer them. They had to go by ambulance, via ferry, over the lake to the regional trauma center. The ones who needed to go were always those fixing to die—septic babies, crashing traumas, bad strokes, risky deliveries.

Ambulance was king. Kurt was the EMS medical director. He provided education and oversight to the EMTs and paramedics. He loved it. They loved him. Until the day when things went bad.

All the ambulances came straight to the ED to offload their patients. It didn't matter if there were sicker patients who'd been waiting for hours and the ambulance was bringing over a hangnail. The ambulance got the available bed.

That made no sense to Emma. *They should get triaged like*

everybody else. The whole point of triage is to decide who's the sickest and needs to be seen first. She talked to Kurt and tried to change the protocols. The change would also curb ambulance overuse by the "frequent flyers," the regulars who knew the rules and took advantage of them.

Kurt disagreed. He wanted his ambulances free as soon as possible. The EMTs had to offload immediately and head back out. "They don't have time to sit around waiting for the triage nurse. Drop them off and go; that's the way."

"They still have to wait to give report to a nurse. The triage nurse will see them faster."

Kurt didn't buy it. He shook his head, clenched his fists in his tight pants, and scowled. "Getting the stretcher into the triage area is complicated. It's difficult, and it takes time."

"The triage nurse can meet them in the ambulance bay. That's going to save time."

"That makes no sense."

She insisted. He got angry. He'd been there longer; he had administrative experience; he was a man.

He may not say it, but she knew damn well that she was only a woman in a man's world. From the patients who called her "Nurse," after she'd just introduced herself as Dr. Steele, to the CEO who called her "Honey" instead of Doctor, and to Kurt here, they all made sure she wouldn't forget that she was just a woman.

She couldn't talk him into it. She couldn't convince Dr. Kenneth Leep, the ED director, either. Maybe because he was Kurt's friend and mentor. Maybe because he just didn't see the point. Maybe because she was wrong, even though she'd seen this work at one of Boston's best-known hospitals. She failed.

Status quo. The ambulances continued to drop their

patients in the ED stretchers no matter what else was going on in the department. Nothing changed. Until one day.

That day, Mrs. Gail Rose, who suffered from anxiety, fibromyalgia, chronic pain, and depression, felt lonely. She needed Dilaudid, her drug of choice. She was one of the regulars. She may have been drug seeking, or maybe not. Nobody but her knew for sure. She was distressed and disturbed, and she knew better than to drive herself to the ED to wait for hours. She called 911 and got an ambulance, her much-needed Dilaudid, and the last open bed.

In the meantime, Mr. Tom Curtis sat patiently in the waiting room. He was sixty-nine and healthy. He was there for indigestion. It had started earlier in the day, as he dug a hole to bury Mocha, his beloved eleven-year-old chocolate Lab.

Mr. Curtis had been waiting for five hours when he suddenly fell to the ground. Joann, his high school sweetheart and his wife of fifty-one years, screamed. The triage nurse called the charge nurse, who pulled Mrs. Rose's stretcher out to make room for Mr. Curtis. They coded him for forty-five minutes, but he stayed as dead as his beloved Mocha. He went to the morgue in a covered stretcher, allowing Mrs. Rose back to her room. Then the questions started. Why? Who? How?

That unfortunate incident, as Kurt called it, caused a lot of discussion about triage protocols—and other things. Somebody remembered Emma trying to change the system and Kurt and Ken disagreeing. That person reminded Kurt about it and also told Administration.

That was not good news.

Mr. Curtis's family sued the hospital for five million dollars for their losses, including lost work and income opportunities for Mr. Curtis, loss of emotional support for his children and grandchildren, and loss of consortium for his wife. Whether Mrs. Curtis's sex life was worth five million dollars or not was debatable. The hospital had to settle for an undisclosed sum of money, and the administration was not pleased. Neither were Ken and Kurt.

Kurt, as always, talked his way out of it, but he resigned the EMS director position and he never forgot. Since that day he had only spoken to Emma when he had to. That was unfortunate, but there was nothing more she could do.

That had been years ago. She wished he'd forget it. He didn't. She wanted to walk out and leave him the room, but she couldn't. It would look like she was afraid of him. *No can do.* She gave him a big smile, then pulled the silly beige curtain between the beds. It was meant to give the patients some privacy, but it did nothing to stop the sound. Unless they needed hearing aids, everybody could hear clearly whatever everybody else said. That made for a good time when people described their sex lives, their discharges, and their bowel movements.

There were no chairs, so Emma pulled out the red hazard disposal bin and sat on it. That made the patients more comfortable and gave her back a little rest.

Kurt glared at her and left. Emma smiled, introduced herself, and started asking questions while proceeding with her evaluation. *She looks comfortable; there's no facial droop; she's moving all extremities; no slurred speech, no increased work of breathing, no fever, no confusion, good eye contact.*

"What were you doing when the headache started? Did it come on suddenly, or did it start gradually and then get worse?" Emma asked, trying to rule out the dangerous headache diagnoses—stroke, meningitis, glaucoma, bleeds.

"I was watching *Jeopardy*. It's just a migraine. I've had migraines for years, and this one is no different." The woman rubbed her right temple with her thumb, massaging away the pain.

That was good news. As Emma proceeded to the neuro exam, her phone vibrated in her pocket. She hoped it was Taylor. Her daughter had been having a hard time since she'd broken up with her boyfriend, Tom, a few months ago. Taylor had come home one day and said, "No more Tom. I don't want to hear his name anymore."

She refused to answer any questions. Emma had wondered if he'd ditched her and Taylor was too proud to admit it. *She hates appearing vulnerable and would rather drown than ask for help.* Her grades started falling, and she became even moodier. She was barely, if ever, home. Emma tried to speak to her again and again, but Taylor would have none of it—she seldom bothered to take her eyes off her phone.

Minerva, Emma's old friend and Taylor's pediatrician, wasn't worried. "That's what happened to Mai. She'd been a wonderful child. We got along great until she turned thirteen and became a monster. Five years of dealing with her felt like fifty. When she turned eighteen, the monster disappeared and Mai came back. It's the raging hormones. It's going to be the same with Taylor."

Minerva is wrong. Emma and Taylor had never gotten along, not even when Taylor was a baby. She'd always preferred her father. When Emma and Victor divorced, Taylor broke up with Emma for good. She didn't speak to her for months. Even now, years later, when the bygones were bygones and Victor and Emma were good friends, Taylor avoided her and ignored her. Something was missing in their relationship. It always had been. Moreover, Taylor was in trouble. Emma didn't know why, but she knew that something was wrong. *Really wrong.*

She shrugged and got back to the present. The headache looked fine. Her neuro exam was on point. Her story was reassuring. Emma decided to skip any further testing. *I'll treat her and street her.*

SPIDER

I'm cold. Been looking for hours.
I find the car in the far parking lot.
A nice one.
I look inside.
A jacket. Books. Not much.
I try the door. It opens.
Stupid!
I slide inside. I open the glove compartment.
Registration?
Yep.
Got his name.
Doing good.

4

EMMA STRETCHED HER BACK. It hurt. She wished she had taken her Motrin. She sighed. The smell of freshly ground coffee hit her, immediately followed by the foul smell of human feces. Code Brown. Somebody didn't make it to the bathroom. *They say ground coffee absorbs the smell. Not really; you just get coffee that smells like shit. Or the other way 'round.* She held her breath until she reached her desk.

An EKG, somebody's heart tracing, sat on the keyboard. She frowned. *The EKG shouldn't be here; they should have brought it to me to read.* It looked OK. The patient was young, only 35. It made a heart attack less likely. They'd call her if he was sick. She signed it and forgot it.

She logged in again, going through the multiple obligatory steps of swiping her ID, putting in her password, her ID number, her PIN, her mother's maiden name, her shoe and bra size, and God only knows what else before she was finally able to place orders for the migraine she'd just seen.

She took a phone call—a referral from the Urgent Care down the road. They were sending a patient over. *What are these urgent care places good for if they can't even deal with a young healthy urinary tract infection? I hope they'll at least send the lab results with her so we don't have to repeat them and charge her again.* She re-paged the intensivist for the kid with the OD, then checked the labs for the sepsis in Room 2. *He's old and sick. He needs antibiotics. Now.* She stood up and unbent, then walked to Sal's desk.

Sal sat with his back extra-straight, as if he were playing the piano. He was the son of musicians. His father played the cello; his mother the violin. He was supposed to become a musician but somehow ended up being a pharmacist. He was smart, pleasant, and single. *I wonder if he's gay.* His long slim fingers danced on the keyboard in a graceful fury, as if he were playing Rachmaninoff, but instead of a concerto he produced the med list for the demented patient in Room 5.

"Sal, could you put in antibiotics for Room 2, for sepsis, please?"

"Sure. Do we know the source?"

"I'm thinking pneumonia, his sats are low. He was in the hospital last month with the same."

"Of course. Dr. Steele, do you have a moment?"

She didn't, not really, but if Sal needed her, she would. She drew up a chair.

"What's up?"

"That code, earlier today... the overdose..."

She looked at him, waiting.

"He got a lot of Narcan."

So that's what's bothering him. It's bothering me too.

"He did."

"I've never given that much Narcan to one patient at one time."

"Neither have I."

"He did look like he responded to it in the end."

"Either that or we were lucky. But I agree, it looks as if it was the Narcan."

"Why?"

"I'm not sure. I read an article about a slew of poorly responsive overdoses in New Hampshire. They thought it was a batch of heroine mixed with fentanyl. Then there was another one, apparently carfentanyl, in Ohio. In some cases, they needed up to twenty-five milligrams to respond."

"That's exactly what I was thinking," Sal said, his face lightening. They were on the same page. "Fentanyl is one hundred times more potent than morphine. It binds tighter to the receptors, so you need more Narcan to make it work."

"That makes sense."

"This isn't the first case like this. There was another one a couple of days ago."

"Who was the doc?"

"Dr. Umber."

Dr. Richard Umber, a slightly older and taller replica of Tom Cruise, stopped by. "Are you taking my name in vain?" he asked smiling, showing his left dimple.

"I was telling Dr. Steele about the overdose you had the other day."

"Which one? They're dropping like flies up here."

Dr. Umber was new to the area. He was a *locum tenens*, a traveling physician working a few shifts here, a few shifts there, as needed. He'd only been with them for a few months, on and off, but he was pleasant, competent, and terribly good-looking.

"The elderly woman in Room 2, the one you gave multiple doses of Narcan before she came through."

"That wasn't an overdose. It was a heart attack," Umber said. "I gave the Narcan just in case—you never know—but it didn't do anything."

"But she did get a pulse after the third dose?"

Dr. Umber dismissed the idea with a flick of his right hand. The red stone of his school ring gleamed like a drop of blood. "Yeah, but that was also after the fourth dose of epi and the second dose of bicarb and the calcium and the magnesium and the CPR. You don't know that it was the Narcan. It could have been any or all of the others. It probably was."

Sal shrugged. Dr. Umber was right; it could have been anything. It could have been just her luck.

"Did you send a drug screen?" Emma asked.

Umber shook his head. "We never even got a urine. She didn't make it through the code. What's the point? Dead is dead." He shrugged and walked away with the smooth, low walk of a big cat.

"It sure looked like an OD though," Sal said.

Emma didn't know what to think. *Sal is awesome, but he's only a pharmacist. Umber is an experienced emergency doc with lots of clinical experience. He must have coded hundreds.*

"Maybe her heart couldn't take the stress," she said. "Or maybe it was an overdose. The one today surely looked like one. We could have a bad batch here, Fentanyl mixed into whatever they're using."

"It makes sense, doesn't it? I read that they make it cheaply in China, and it's easy to bring over since it's so potent that a little goes a long way. They mix it with all sorts of adulterants to sell it. Maybe they put in a little too much, or maybe our folks aren't used to it and they don't know how much to use and then end up with unintentional overdoses."

"It makes sense. I'll send his urine for a drug screen and see what shows up."

"I'll make sure we get some extra Narcan in here," Sal

said. "I had to run down to pharmacy for the last two doses. We shouldn't need to do that on top of everything else."

"Thanks, Sal. I'll run that drug screen, and I'll let you know."

"I'll call the Poison Control Center. I have a friend working there; I'll have a chat with her."

Emma stood up and straightened. *It hurts. I wish this shift was over so I could go home and find out about Taylor. And rest. And have a drink. Four more hours.*

She looked at Sal staring at his screen, his back straight, his slim hands flying over the keyboard.

"Sal, why did you quit the piano?"

His eyes widened in surprise. "I didn't quit. I still play."

"But you dropped it as a career when you decided to be a pharmacist rather than a musician. Why?"

Sal looked at his hands, then back at her. "I wanted to make the world a better place. I thought that as a pharmacist I could help people."

"Musicians help people too. They bring beauty and solace to the world."

"Yes. But people have to first be healthy and free of pain to enjoy music and beauty."

Emma nodded.

Sal asked, "Isn't that why you chose to be a doctor? To help people?"

She laughed. "No, not me. That's what they all say to get into medical school, but that's bullshit. If I weren't here to care for these patients, somebody else would. Somebody faster and better than me. Nobody is irreplaceable; I sure am not."

"It's hard to believe."

"Thank you. That's nice to hear. I became a doctor for the challenge. I enjoy the thrill of finding the answers, the search for a diagnosis. Like a detective looking for the killer, I love the chase. I also love the procedures. I didn't do it for them," she said, nodding toward the hallways packed with stretchers after all the rooms had been filled. "I did it for me."

"Well, lucky them, anyhow. And lucky us."

"Thank you." Emma smiled. *I can use a little love.*

SPIDER

I'm sitting on the bench by the door.
Waiting.
People go in. People come out. None of them is him.
I'm cold. I can't feel my toes. Gone for half an hour now.
My fingers too.
I tighten my fists in my pockets.
My coat's wet. Not warm. Nothing's warm.
I shiver.
It's been an hour now.
"He'll be done in half an hour," they said an hour ago.
"I wanna thank him," I said. "I wanna thank him properly for
what he did for me."
I show them my package. Long, white, spruced with a
golden bow.
It's a gift.
They don't know what's inside. I do.
The fat one with the bad teeth smiles.
"He'll be out soon. I'll tell him you're waiting."
"No, no, don't. I wanna surprise him."
"I see."

She doesn't.
I wait until my fists can't open anymore.
I'm so frozen I couldn't open the box to get the knife.
Tonight's not gonna work.
I head out.
I'll be back tomorrow.

5

EMMA GOT HOME PAST MIDNIGHT. She was frozen and tired. Her neck was killing her. Her bag was heavy with her uneaten lunch and her never-without essentials: scalpel, rubber gloves, flashlight, an alligator forceps to remove tiny things from narrow spaces, a tourniquet to stop bleeding, a few other bits and pieces, and a couple of her favorite medical books. She dropped the bag on the corner chair that used to be Victor's.

She straightened her back, grateful for the warmth embracing her. She'd been cold ever since she left home in the morning. The air-conditioning in the ED was the only thing that never stopped working, summer or winter.

She looked at the pile of dirty dishes in the sink. She didn't know if she was mad or happy. *The kid is home and safe. The sloth could have cleaned the kitchen after herself. I should wake her up to deal with her mess... but do I really want to argue with her now?*

She looked at the wine rack. This was the best moment of her day, choosing her wine and enjoying it. Waking

Taylor would be a fight. She had no more fight left in her tonight. She shrugged. It wasn't worth it.

She went to the rack to choose a bottle. *Chianti? Too rough. Pinot noir? Too weak. Sancerre? Too cold. Malbec? Perfect. It's going to be a Malbec night. That will warm me up nicely.* Yesterday's bottle of Shiraz was in the trash.

She took a long sip, then another. The wine was dry and smooth. It did smell like dry cherries, just like the label said, but she didn't taste any leather. *Just as well. I don't care much for leather in my wine, only in my shoes.* It warmed her inside as she finished the glass. The tension in her shoulders eased.

She started running a scalding hot bath, poured herself another glass, and then turned on the news for company. She checked her email. Work related mostly, a few beautiful Russian brides, an amazing male enhancement cream, a Nigerian philanthropist offering her money. Somebody asking her to save the planet.

I'd love to help, especially with the polar bears, but saving the planet is too tall an order for me the way I'm feeling these days. I'm lucky if I can help Taylor.

She refilled her glass and walked to Taylor's room. Syncopated hip-hop music was coming through the door, the bass loud enough to make her insides shake. She knocked. No answer. She knocked again, then opened the door. Taylor was asleep, her dark hair falling over her face, a heavy book resting on her stomach. Emma picked it up—it was the second Harry Potter, the book that Taylor kept returning to whenever she was upset.

She sat on the chair by the bed and watched her strange, awful, beautiful daughter's slow and steady breathing, her heart torn between love and pain. *She's home, in her bed, safe, at least for tonight.* She remembered the kid she'd coded earlier today—no, it was yesterday by now; it felt like an eternity ago.

His urine had tested positive for fentanyl. Sal had called poison control. They agreed that the fentanyl was a possibility, but had nothing else to offer. Emma hoped the police would do better.

A detective had come to the ED to speak to her. He showed her the pill bottle they had collected at his home. *That would explain why there were no track marks. He wasn't injecting, he was using pills.* The bottle was under his room-mate's name, and it was empty.

He'd made it to the ICU. *Is he going to pull through? Who knows? His brain was starved of oxygen for God knows how long after his heart stopped. At least he could be an organ donor*, Emma thought, with the pragmatic ruthlessness that working in the ED teaches you.

She felt sorry for him and his family. There were so many that she felt sorry for every day, so many who could use his kidneys, his liver, his heart, his lungs, his corneas, his skin, and even bones, and live a better life.

She still hoped he was going to pull through. She was invested in him after that code. She had a daughter who could have been in his place. Fortunately, she wasn't. Not yet.

She turned off the lights, turned down the music, closed the door gently, and went back to the sofa where her friend, the Malbec, was waiting.

She remembered the bath.

Too late.

6

DR. KURT CRUMP hadn't had a good day. As a matter of fact, he hadn't had a good day in a while. Working alongside Emma Steele, that know-it-all, didn't help any. Seeing the nurses swoon over her drove him nuts. "Dr. Steele said... Dr. Steele did... Dr. Steele doesn't think..." Who the hell cared what Dr. Steele thought?

The whole day had sucked, from the drug seekers lying to him, to the demented patient the family wanted resuscitated at any cost. They'd worked on him for an hour before sending him to the ICU to die. Then this Umber guy giving him lip for the sign-out, after he'd stayed two hours over, just because he signed out that non-ambulatory back pain that he couldn't send home.

He walked to the far end of the parking lot where he'd parked his red Audi A7 and unlocked the door. The sight of the beautiful, cream-colored, soft leather seats and the new-car smell should have made him feel better. They didn't.

The radio was on. Madonna's "Material Girl" startled him. He turned her off. He wasn't in the mood for music. He didn't care about the news, either. He really didn't want to hear anything. After fourteen hours spent in the ER chaos, his ears rang with the beeps of the monitors, the screaming patients, the crackling speakers summoning him somewhere. He could do with some silence for a change.

There wasn't going to be any peace at home. He thought about going elsewhere, anywhere. Sheila had been in a foul mood lately; she wasn't going to be any better tonight when he got home three hours late. He hadn't called from work. He didn't have another fight in him. He didn't want to hear her endless questions: "Where are you? Who are you with? Why are you late? When are you leaving? Are you coming directly home?"

He'd texted her: "Leaving now," then turned off the phone. He didn't expect a pleasant reception.

He was right. She'd been crying; he knew it the moment he opened the door and saw her, eyes red and swollen, the smudged mascara making her look like the Joker. She gave him a death stare.

"Where have you been?"

"Where do I look like I've been?" He pointed to his clothes, fresh this morning, now crumpled and stained from a long day of wear. There was some vomit on the trousers and maybe blood on the left sleeve. What else? He didn't want to know.

"Your shift was over three hours ago."

"Tell that to the patients, will you?" he snapped, slamming the bathroom door behind him.

He dropped his shirt in the laundry basket, did the same with his pants and his underwear and everything else he wore except for the tie. It was his favorite Armani tie. The deep blue of the peacock feathers brought out the blue of his eyes, Kayla said.

He looked at it, smelled it, and dropped it in the garbage

bin. He took a long, hot shower to wash away the misery, the pain, the dirt, and the rest of this trying day, one of many. The scalding hot water felt good and clean. Liberating. He forced himself to turn off the shower. He dried himself with an old blue towel, put on his well-worn navy flannel pajamas, and resigned himself to facing his fate.

She was still seething.

"Why did you have to stay three hours past your shift?"

"Because I had to finish seeing and dispoeing my patients." He poured himself a glass of Redbreast Irish Whiskey, no water, no ice. The smooth burn of the Single Pot Still in his mouth helped him feel better.

"Why didn't you sign them out?"

"I did, but I had to see them first. They'd been there for hours."

"I don't believe you."

She choked with sobs, her mouth fish-ugly as it curved down. He looked past her at their wedding picture, a long-lost time when she was pretty and smiling.

They were happy.

That was long ago.

"You went to see her," she wailed, hugging her knees. Her brown hair with dirty white roots fell over her face.

She looks like an old witch, he thought, and took another sip.

"I didn't. I'm coming from work."

"Then you saw her there!" she wailed again. "Stop lying and at least admit it. Be a man!"

He wondered what he could say to make this stop.

Nothing, probably. She'd go on and on until she ran out of steam.

After her second miscarriage, she had become pathologically jealous. She felt that she was worthless if she couldn't bear his children. She thought that any other woman could replace her. She became more and more demanding. She called him at work when she knew damn well that he didn't have time for this. She sat at the same side of the table with him at restaurants to see who he was looking at. She drove to the hospital to see if his car was still in the parking lot.

He'd tried to reassure her. He had put up with her demands, hoping she'd finally understand that he wasn't cheating on her. He wasn't interested in other women.

It didn't help.

Then he met Kayla.

Kayla was young and pretty. Kayla was funny, and she never cried. She had lustrous chestnut hair falling to her waist and the figure of a runway model.

Kayla liked him back. She never asked for anything. She was happy with what he could give her, which, between work and Sheila, wasn't much. Kayla made him smile. With her, he felt like a man still worth looking at.

Kayla was everything that Sheila no longer was. His heart soared at the thought of her. But she was far away, and Sheila was here.

He took the last sip of whiskey and held it on his tongue to let the heat seep in. He swallowed and took a deep breath. He sat on the couch beside Sheila and forced himself to put his arms around her. He held her quietly.

He thought about her, about Kayla, about Emma. He thought about his old patient who had died earlier, demented and alone.

He held her shaking body until the sobs stopped.

"Let's go to bed."

He lay awake for a long time, thinking about the mess their lives had become. This wasn't what they planned. She had been young and pretty and full of hope.

They had met at an art exhibition. He showed his spring watercolors. She displayed pottery, in curious, inexplicable shapes. He gathered his courage and asked her what the penis-looking thing was.

"Why, a cup of course!"

Her laughter had gone straight to his heart. He'd taken her to dinner, then to bed. They had never looked back.

Is it too late for us?

SPIDER

"He's not on."

They're lying. "He told me to come back tonight. He said he'll be on after 3," I say, smiling like I like them.

Fuck them. Fuck them all.

"He's not," says the fat one with the droopy mouth. She rechecks the papers.

"No, not tonight. You've got it wrong."

I shrink under her gaze. I take out the package. I show it to her. "I got this for him."

The package is tired. I've been carrying it around. I got it squished under my arm so many times it's shaped like my armpit. It's still white-like, but the bow's about to fall off.

It looks secondhand. It is. I found it in a garbage bin. It smells it too, like smoke and booze and sweat.

Never mind, the knife inside it is sharp. I checked. I sliced through a tree branch with a flick of the wrist. It's an old hunting knife shaped like a fish, its scaly handle growing into a long, smooth, solid blade thick enough to cut through ribs.

I'm the hunter. I'm gonna get my kill.

Tonight or tomorrow, I'm gonna get him.

I make myself small. They like it when you're small. Makes them feel big and strong.

I bend my good right knee a bit more and slump my shoulders.

"Got it wrong then. Sorry. When's he on?"

She looks at me, her sharp eyes getting soft. I don't matter; I'm nothing to worry about. I'm small and old and dirty. She's sorry for me.

"I can't tell you," she says. "It's against the rules."

I rub my left eye, the one with the infection. It tears. "I just wanna thank him," I say. "He helped my son; he's a great doctor." I look down and make myself smaller. "I have a gift for him." I show her the box again.

She breaks. She looks at the papers and says, "Tomorrow. Tomorrow at 9. He'll be here."

I rub my eye and thank her. I leave slowly, limping on the left like I always do.

I don't rush until I'm out in the dark and I know she can't see me. They can't see me.

Tomorrow at nine.

7

EMMA SCRUTINIZED THE X-RAY, sliding the magnifier over the lungs, looking for the markings to go all the way to the edge. They did.

The screams came first. "You motherfuckers! I'll have my lawyer arrest you all!"

Then came the stretcher. The man handcuffed to it was squirming and spitting. Two policemen and two sweating EMTs were struggling to hold him down. The uniformed security guards by Room 8 were ready, gloves on, Tasers on their hips.

Emma looked up to see Judy following the stretcher, soft restraints under one arm, blue paper scrubs under the other.

"Mine?" Emma asked.

"Yes."

Emma followed.

"Let me go, you assholes!" the man shouted. His navy sweater was torn. His bruised left elbow peeked out. His heavy, off-black pants were unzipped. The crotch was wet.

No underwear. Boots, no socks. Not enough clothes for the sharp cold.

His purple left eye was swollen shut. The blood around his mouth had dried, but more bloody spit sprayed out with every curse.

"Let's get him a mask. What's his story?"

The black officer holding down his right leg used to be one of their EMTs.

"Good to see you, Dr. Steele. We found him asleep in the doorway at the dollar store. He smells like he's had a few drinks and he looks like he's been in a fight, but he won't answer our questions. Tried to bite us on the way. He spat at the EMTs. Didn't get them though."

"Do we know him? Any history?"

"I'm getting it," Judy said. "He's been here before." She bent over to cover his mouth with the mask. He tried to bite her. She pulled back. He missed.

He launched into another stream of slurred obscenities, struggling to break free. The EMTs held him down. A dozen gloved hands lifted him to drop him on the ER stretcher.

"Five and 2?" Judy asked.

"Great idea," Emma said, "and 25 of Benadryl."

Judy nodded and went to get it. The "5 and 2," the classic "agitation cocktail," 5 mg of Haldol, an antipsychotic, and 2 mg of Ativan, a sedative, could be given in one smooth shot, through the clothes if need be, to sedate agitated patients and keep them, and the staff, safe. *I don't know many things that work better than Haldol, thank God and whoever invented it, and the Ativan is a nice touch. They should make this guy feel much better. Me too.*

"You need help?"

Emma looked up into the smiling, water-colored eyes of

Dr. Dick Umber. His blinding-white coat and his perfect steel-gray hair showing off his Caribbean tan made Emma feel like a shabby mess. *How on earth does he do that? It's like nobody ever spits at him! That's unreal!* She swallowed her envy and smiled back.

"I'm good, thank you." He was handsome, helpful, and smelled bitter-green, like wild carnations. He was the best-looking thing she'd seen all day.

"You'll have to scan him, you know. He looks like he's gotten into some trauma."

"Yes, I know." She was irked at being treated like an intern, but he was right, of course. The guy was drunk, belligerent, and hard to evaluate. Putting him through the scanner was going to be a challenge, but she didn't need him to tell her that.

"I had a guy like that in Colorado Springs. He'd hit a tree skiing. No helmet. We all thought he was drunk. He was acting so drunk that he could barely speak. His blood alcohol was zero, but he had a head bleed the size of an orange in his frontal lobe. He was so altered that we had to tube him to get him in the scanner."

Emma wasn't looking forward to that, but she might have to do it if the Haldol didn't work. The patient needed to be perfectly still for a couple of minutes to get the scan. Not likely.

"I may have to do that. Let's see how this works."

"What would you use?"

"Ketamine, probably."

"For a head injury?"

So he's old school and not up to date. Who'd have thunk? Ketamine, also known as Special K or K-hole by its many fans, was often used to sedate horses—and people. A cousin to PCP, maligned for decades and forbidden in people with head injuries for fear that it would increase the intracranial pressure and squish the brain out. Not true. Newer research showed that Ketamine actually helped in brain injury. The old-timers didn't know it though, unless they kept abreast of the news.

She wouldn't have thought him an old-timer, but he must have been in his late forties, so maybe twenty years out of medical school? He was quite the show-off, she'd heard. The nurses liked him, and he liked them back, especially the young and pretty ones. They liked his stories about sailing around the world and escaping sharks and climbing down mountains on broken legs. Quite an adventurer, Dr. Umber, but not so keen on the latest in medicine.

"Yes. Haven't you heard? Ketamine is the cat's ass now. They use it in head injuries and for sedation in psychotics and even for seizures and depression. Ketamine is the new black." She smiled and turned back to her patient.

"Hey, Emma, what are you doing tonight? Wanna go for a drink after work?"

Is this a date? Or just a friendly "Let's chill together after work" thing? She hadn't been on a date since... last summer? Or maybe the one before that? And no matter what it was, should she go drinking and then drive home? But then he was funny and handsome and smelled good, and she hadn't been out in ages. She could take a taxi... or maybe he'd give her a ride.

She smiled at him with new warmth. "Why not?"

"A few nurses and I will be at The Apple at six. Come chill with us."

Not a date, after all. Getting involved with a colleague was a bad idea, but she hadn't felt attractive in so long she could have used a boost. She was a doctor, a mother, a housekeeper, in that order. Being a woman was not on the list.

"Thanks, I'll see how things line up."

8

———

THE FIRST "5 AND 2" didn't do much, but the second shot put him to sleep. They rushed him through the scanner. No bleed. Emma checked him out thoroughly. No badness beyond the bruises. Relieved, she left him sleeping and went back to her desk.

Ken, the ED director, was waiting for her. No white coat. *Office work for him today. It must be nice.*

"How is he?"

"He's fine; he just needs to sleep it off. How are you?"

"I'm OK. Busy today?"

"As usual. We're full here. Seven more in triage."

"Can you stop by for a moment?" She looked at the line of stretchers in the hallways, all full, and then looked back at him. He waited. *It must be important.*

"I'll be there."

She sat in the guest chair in Ken's office, staring at the open door behind him. *How can he sit with his back to an open door? Anybody passing by can look at him and at his computer screen without him even knowing. That's crazy! I walk out of*

restaurants when I can't sit with my back against the wall! I'm
paranoid, but he's not paranoid enough!

She looked at his kind, tired face. For once he wasn't
smiling. Something was wrong.

"What did I do this time?" she joked.

"They didn't tell me yet." He stood up and closed the
door. "This is a private conversation."

Emma nodded.

"It's about Kurt. I need your help."

That's odd. Kurt is no friend of mine, and Ken knows it.

"Sheila, his wife, thinks that Kurt is having an affair with
Kayla and that he's getting ready to leave her. She says Kurt
bought Kayla a new car."

Emma pulled her feet under her chair, hoping it was
going to be over soon.

"If that's true, it's not only a tragedy for them but an
administrative problem. Kurt is Kayla's superior. In these
#MeToo times, when even an innocent joke can be
perceived as sexual harassment, this is a ticking bomb. This
will reflect poorly not only on him but on the whole ED. I
thought about talking to him, but it's difficult. We have years
of friendship that I don't want to jeopardize. Would you
speak to Kayla? She likes you and trusts you."

That's weird. "I have no authority to ask Kayla anything
about her personal life. We aren't close friends. You want me
to ask her if she's sleeping with Kurt?"

"You can do better than that. As for authority, I recommended you for the position of ED assistant director."

"Assistant director? How about Kurt?"

"Kurt will continue to be an ED attending."

"But nothing's been proven yet! How about due process?"

"Kurt has had previous issues. Administration had

already considered replacing him. This is just the last straw."

"What did he do?"

"I can't tell you."

"He won't like this."

"I know. There's nothing I can do. As a matter of fact, my days on the job are numbered. I expect to be fired any day. I'm just trying to clear up this mess before they throw me out."

"I'm so sorry."

"Me too. For the last twenty-five years I've given my life to this place. I didn't expect it to end up like this. This place has no soul." He started shuffling papers on his desk, avoiding her eyes. His hunched shoulders spelled defeat, and his large, knotty hands trembled.

"What are you going to do?"

"I'll retire. I've been thinking about that for a while, but I couldn't bring myself to do it. They've made it easy. I'll finally have enough time to go fishing and hiking. I'll read the books I've been putting off for years. I'll spend more time with my wife. I'm almost looking forward to it." He looked her in the eye and asked, "The real question is: What are *you* going to do?"

"I need to think." *This is the opportunity I've been waiting for. This would boost my career and set me up for further promotions. But there's Taylor. I don't have much time for Taylor as it is; on the other hand, Taylor is turning eighteen and she'll be leaving for college.*

"I think I'll take the job. What do you think?"

There was kindness and pity in Ken's eyes. When he spoke, his words came out like splinters.

"Emma, I've known you for years. You're bright, tough, and hardworking. I wish I had more docs like you. You're ambitious and dedicated. That's why I floated your name. I know you'll do a great job. I just hope you won't get crushed in the process.

"Kurt will hate you even more than he does. The others too. Their friends in the department will make your life miserable. They'll get rid of me, and that will make things even worse. You'll be the scapegoat for everything that doesn't work. You'll be the punching bag for the doctors when they don't like the schedule or the support services fail or the computer system goes down, and the punching bag for the administration whenever there's a complaint. Whatever goes wrong will be your fault."

"You sure know how to talk me into it." Emma tried to lighten the mood.

"Whatever they tell you, this is a full-time job and then some. 24/7 on call. Whatever happens, whenever it happens, it's your problem. They'll call you if things get bad, if somebody gets sick or forgets to show up for work—whatever happens, it's all you. I'm an old man with not much of a life. You're a woman and a mother. Shouldn't you spend more time with Taylor instead?"

Emma hung her head. She was about to put her career ahead of her daughter. Again.

"Thank you, Ken. You're right. I'll think about it."

She went back to the ED.

They were waiting.

9

———

EMMA WAS late to the Apple. She had met with Victor and Taylor's counselor.

Taylor was skipping classes. She was moody and difficult. She was giving her teachers a rough time. She was failing classes. She'd failed to even turn in her English homework, she, the best writer in her class.

"She's hanging out with the wrong crowd," Ms. Perkins said, looking at them over her round glasses. Paired with her stringy gray hair, they made her look like the wicked witch of the West.

Emma shrunk, raised her shoulders, and drew her feet under her chair, assuming her guilty posture. She'd done it as a child whenever her mother blew up. She was still doing it, thirty years later.

"She'll grow out of it." Victor shrugged. "She's just a kid."

He was annoyed that he had to carve time out of his busy day for this. Rocking in his chair, he looked like a kid himself, with his unruly curly hair, his pout, and his muddy boots.

"She's seventeen. She's no longer a kid," Emma said.

Victor had always been too lenient with Taylor. *He's her best friend more than he's her father. That leaves me to be the bad guy, the only one to ever say no. No wonder Taylor wants to leave home and move in with him.*

That worried her. Between Victor's schedule—on call every fourth night and every fourth weekend—and his lenience, Taylor would go completely unsupervised. *Sure, Amber's there, but Amber is barely older than Taylor—what is she, 29?—and she's busy taking care of her own kids. Not to mention the hairdresser, pedicures, and shopping. I bet Victor isn't helping much. He likes playing with his kids, but disciplining them? No.*

"She'll be of age in one year."

"She's exactly as I was at her age. She's got to have some fun. If not now, then when?"

"You got straight A's when you were her age. You were polite and loving to your parents, no matter what else you did. She's failing three subjects. She's a pain to deal with at home. Take my word for it."

"She just needs a little time. She never got over that business with Tom."

"Did she tell you about Mike?" Ms. Perkins asked.

"Who's Mike?" Victor asked, checking his watch.

"Mike was one of Taylor's friends. Nice kid. Troubled. He died last week."

"Died? How?" asked Emma.

"Drug overdose, apparently."

Emma and Victor looked at each other.

That was beyond skipping classes and acting like a teenager. If her friends were doing drugs, Taylor may be too. That would explain her sudden change, her rotten mood, and her poor school performance.

"Did you know about this?" Victor asked Emma.

"Of course not. She never speaks to me, as you are well aware. Did *you* know?"

"No, I didn't."

His body slumped. The chair rocked forward, resting on all its feet. The carefree kid disappeared. A worried father took his place.

Emma wished she could feel sorry for him, but she was too angry. *It's his fault that Taylor is unmanageable.*

"We don't know that she's using, though," he said. "We shouldn't jump to conclusions. For all that we know, this has nothing to do with her."

"So what do you suggest? Wait and see if we find her dead?"

Victor looked her in the eye.

"You didn't really mean that; you're just upset. I am too, but there is no point in ripping into each other. We need to work together."

He was right, of course, but she was too mad to think. She took a long deep breath, opened her mouth to speak, and then closed it tight enough for her jaw to hurt.

"I'll speak to her," he said.

"What are you going to tell her?"

"I don't know." He took off his glasses to wipe them clean with slow circular motions using the bottom of his shirt, like he always did when he had to make a difficult decision.

She remembered him proposing to her, eons ago. Then too, he'd taken off his glasses. He'd wiped them clean with the bottom of his short white coat that all medical students wore. *He used to be young and handsome, his jet-black hair curling around his ears, his smiling eyes ocean blue. We were both medical students. We were ready to take on the world. Invincible. Now? We're old, our marriage is dead, and we're about to fail our only child.* Her heart ached for all the things they'd lost: youth, love, marriage.

"You want to talk to her together?"

"Good idea," Ms. Perkins said. "Show a united front."

She thinks Victor won't push Taylor, but she knows that I will.

They walked out together and stopped near Emma's red Hyundai.

"How about tomorrow?" Emma asked. She opened the door and dropped her bag on top of the green jacket Taylor had left on the passenger seat.

"Not tomorrow. Sunday? I can be there by nine, before she wakes up and takes off."

Emma nodded. He turned to leave.

He took two steps and turned around, his fists tight in the pockets of his old jeans.

"Should we have her tested?" he asked, staring at his muddy boots.

"How would that help?"

"At least we'd know for sure whether she's using or not."

"We wouldn't. We don't even know what to test her for. A lot of drugs won't show in the usual drug tests. Plus there's so much cross-reactivity that she could test positive even if she didn't use anything—like testing positive for amphetamines after taking decongestants." This was her field. She knew it inside-out, just like he knew his cardiology stuff.

"Why don't we ask her first?"

He nodded and walked away.

Emma started her car. She sat, watching his tail lights fade.

He's going home to Amber and the girls. He'll get dinner, company, and love. He's even got the dogs. I'm going home to

nothing. Unless Taylor's home. Then it's even worse. Like the
night he told me.

It was years ago, but she still remembered every sound,
every taste, every shadow.

10

THE ONLY LIGHT was in the kitchen. Emma wondered why. It was late, past Taylor's bedtime, and Victor barely knew where to find the kitchen.

Is she sick?

She pulled in. She parked too close to Victor's Subaru, but she was too tired to care. Her nine-hour shift had turned into twelve. She had nothing left inside.

The cold had gotten into her bones. *I hate the air-conditioning. They must be doing it on purpose, so that the living don't get too comfortable and the dead don't rot.* She shivered, looking forward to a hot bath to wash off the grime and the misery of her many patients since this morning. Yesterday morning now.

She walked to the kitchen.

Victor read at the kitchen table, empty but for a bouquet of roses and an open bottle of red wine. The roses made the kitchen look both festive and foreign.

"You're late," he said, pouring wine into a pair of long-stem glasses and handing her one.

Emma did a mental check. Anniversary? Birthday? Mother's Day?

She lifted her glass and watched the light struggling to flow through its dark redness. *It's thick as blood.* She sniffed it, then swirled it for a second nose. The darkness was there too, the bitter cherry flavor and licorice and maybe violets, a rich bouquet of wildflowers and dark fruit, spelling money.

She took a sip. She let it flow under her tongue, then behind her teeth, striking the remotest taste buds. The acid, the tannins, and the floral bitterness made them sing.

"Nice wine," she said. She sat, pulling her jacket around her.

She eyed the flowers. A dozen red roses with baby's breath and greens, spilling out from their only vase. Their glamour clashed with the peeling cabinets and the chipped sink. The kitchen was empty. Everything was put away. That never happened—neither she nor Victor were the house-keeping type—and as for Taylor, she was the child goddess of entropy.

Sports jacket past midnight. He's looking tired. Even his curls look flat. His periwinkle eyes, red-rimmed behind his glasses, didn't meet hers. Her heart skipped. She opened her mouth to ask.

She didn't.

She took another sip of wine instead.

Victor sat his glass on the table, took off his glasses, and started cleaning them with his shirt, like he always did when collecting his thoughts. He blew on the lenses and wiped them with slow circular movements, without looking up.

It's not Taylor. It's something else, and it's bad.

"Emma, you know how important you are to me."

It's worse than bad. Emma finished her glass and poured

herself another. She picked up the bottle and checked the label. Chateau Pavie, St. Emilion, 1999. Good vintage. Excellent in fact.

"Taylor too."

Her brain splintered and burned. *Divorce. That's what's happening. I didn't see it coming.*

She thought back about the last few months. He'd been away a lot. She'd been busy herself, between the ED shifts, the house, and Taylor. This was the first time they were sharing a bottle of wine this year. As for the flowers…

"Nice flowers."

He blushed.

She looked into the living room for clues. Nothing there. She recalled the vague shape of boxes in his car.

More wine.

"I'm leaving."

"Where to?"

"I'm leaving you."

Emma nodded.

"You're not making it easy!"

Emma laughed. "Where are you going?"

"Where? Don't you want to know why?"

"I imagine you found a better option."

"I'm expecting a baby."

"Congratulations! You may get a Nobel prize for that!"

Victor's eyes finally connected. "I'm sorry, Emma."

"That's too bad. You should be excited."

"I'm sorry about doing this to you."

"How about Taylor?"

"I'm very sorry about Taylor too!"

"Me too. You're taking her."

"Taking her? Taking her where?"

"With you."

The shock on Victor's face was fun to watch. *Almost.*

"I can't take her with me!"

"Why not? She's your daughter, just like this child you're expecting."

"But..."

"But what?"

"You're her mother!"

"I couldn't help but notice. And you're her father."

"She needs to be with you!"

"Did you ask her?"

"No."

"You should. She'd rather be with you."

"But she's only eight! She doesn't know what's best for her!"

"And you do?"

"Don't you want her?"

"No."

"Why not?"

"Like you, I have better things to do."

"But she's your daughter!"

Emma laughed. "She's yours too, remember?"

"You're kidding, aren't you?"

"Not at all."

"But I'm busy! I have my work and my patients and..."

Emma waited.

"And Amber's pregnant!"

Emma remembered Amber. *Young, pretty, girly. Giggled a lot. She rotated through the ED in nursing school, then she got a job in Cardiology. The rest is history.* Emma tried to not be bitter. She failed. *Giggly, girly Amber, twelve years younger, took Victor and destroyed my marriage.*

"It's going to be good practice for her to take care of a child. At least this one is potty-trained. As for busy, I'm just as busy as you are. I have my shifts and my patients. I'm in no better shape to take care of Taylor than you are. I'll keep the dogs."

Victor's mouth narrowed into a thin line.

"Listen, Emma, if this is your way of taking revenge..."

"Where are we going, Daddy?" Taylor asked. She stood in the open door with Dora, her rag doll, under her arm. Her faded pink blanket dragged behind her, like it had been since she'd started walking. She had Victor's dark curls falling over her fierce eyes. She was packed and ready to go.

"To bed, sweetheart. We're going to bed now." Victor picked her up—Dora, blanket, and all—and took her to her bedroom.

Emma sat in the empty kitchen. She focused on the wine, on its red glow in the crystal glass, on its full-bodied flavor, on the smoothness of the stem. She pushed aside the emptiness, the murmur of the bedside story in Taylor's room, the guilt in Victor's eyes.

Tomorrow.

She kept pressure on the thought of tomorrow like she'd keep pressure on a bleeding wound.

For tonight, she'd just stay alive.

Tomorrow.

Nine years ago and it still hurts.

They didn't tell Taylor until weeks later, when they returned from their last family vacation. Victor had taken the dogs, of course, and Emma ended up with Taylor. *What a deal!* She shook her head and headed home. Two minutes later she changed her mind. She turned around in the hospital parking lot to drive to The Apple.

SPIDER

It's getting dark.
He's coming. Heading to the car.
I follow like the whisper of a shadow.
Going to the far parking lot. Good.
The farther the better.
I close in, right hand in my pocket, making love to the handle.
I love this knife. She loves me.
He's by the car. I step forward to grab him.
The lights hit him. A car. It stops next to him.
The window opens.
A woman.
Brown-haired, white coat, scrubs. Smiling.
"Emma!" he says.
She looks at me sharply.
One step and I melt in the dark.
I move on.
I'll be back.

11

THEY WERE STILL THERE. After a few drinks, they were laughing and speaking all over each other in the private back room.

Umber was whispering in Kayla's ear, his golden tan set off by his sweater in the color of deep water. Judy, still in scrubs, was laughing with George, who looked like a satyr with flushed olive skin. Kelly was chatting with Nora, the new, pretty CNA who looked a little out of place sitting on the other side of Dick.

Their cheerful welcome filled her heart. It felt good to be wanted. These were her people, more than her own family. With them, she belonged.

Sal moved aside to make room for her. She sat between him and Kelly.

"I'm glad you made it," Dick said, pouring her a generous glass of wine. "To good friends!"

Emma raised her glass and took a sip. The wine was good, dry, robust, and a little rough, like most Chiantis are. She thanked him, but she didn't fail to notice that he'd poured her wine without asking.

Mr. Macho Man had decided for her.

"Good to see you, Dr. Steele," Kayla said, prettier than ever with her wine-flushed cheeks and sparkling eyes.

"Good to see you, Kayla."

Emma liked her easy smile and outgoing personality almost as much as she appreciated her competency. She was an ED clerk, the hub of communication with the other departments. She made things happen with a smile, even when she had to deal with grumpy surgeons and irate family members. She was a gem.

I hope the rumors about Kurt and her are false. She deserves better.

Dick refilled Kayla's glass, though it didn't need it. "This wine's not bad, but it's not as good as mine. Did I tell you about my vineyard in Languedoc? Great terroir. We make a nice dry red."

"Really? You own a winery? In France?"

"A small one. Just one thousand bottles per year."

"Who looks after it?" Emma asked.

"The old Frenchman I bought it from. His wife died, and he had to sell. I offered to let him live there in exchange for managing the place and a little cash. It's been one of the best deals I've ever made.

Dick took another sip of wine and rested his arm on the back of Kayla's chair. "Too bad that I don't get to spend much time there between my work and my boat."

"You have a boat too?" Kayla asked.

"I bought this Sun Odyssey 49. I'm keeping it in a marina in Mazatlán to get it refurbished. I'll have to take you sailing some day. It should be ready by June."

"You sail it yourself? Where?"

"Looking at transatlantic crossings. Thinking about starting a business of themed sailing vacations. I'll get an

Iron Chef to give cooking lessons, or a yogini to lead a medi-
tation cruise, or a yoga retreat, something like that."

Kayla looked at him in awe.

Kelly elbowed Emma and rolled her eyes. "Wait until he
gets around to saving the Dalai Lama's life," she whispered,
loud enough for him to hear.

Emma choked. "How do you manage to do all this and
still work?"

"I delegate. I have people who do it for me. I'm flying to
Mexico in a couple of weeks to check on the boat progress.
Wanna come?" he asked Kayla.

She smiled.

Emma hoped she wasn't taking him seriously. He had
shifty eyes. No wonder Ken was thinking about getting rid of
him. "He's too much trouble. He can't see a girl without
going after her." Emma had tried to talk him out of it, but
Ken had had it. "Yeah, I know he's a good doctor when he's
not in bed with one of the nurses. I warned him twice.
That's it. Next time he's gone!"

Kelly intervened. "She knows better than to trust a
charmer like you. Where do you live?"

"I have a winter place in Colorado, near Aspen. I love
skiing."

"I love skiing too," Nora said.

Dick took another sip of wine.

"And in summer?"

"Oh, here and there. Mostly out and about, working."

"How long have you been doing locums work?" Kayla
asked.

"Almost seven years."

"It's got to be hard to have no home to go to at night, no
kitchen, no pets," Nora said.

Umber shrugged. "It's good money. It gives you an

opportunity to meet new people." He turned toward Kayla and raised his glass. "And pretty girls like you!"

Nora stood up so fast that her chair fell backward. "Good night, everybody. I have to go."

That was abrupt. Is she one of the names Dick crossed off his list, upset now that he's flirting with Kayla?

"I hope she's OK," Kayla said.

They started talking again, but the easy banter was gone.

Emma turned to Sal, quietly sipping his beer. "What's new with you?"

"Not much." His voice went down a notch. "That kid. The code the other day, the one who needed all that Narcan..."

"Yes?"

"I checked his medical history. The meds bottle wasn't his; it was his girlfriend's. She got four opiate prescriptions last month."

"Any of them fentanyl?"

"None. That's what makes it so interesting. Whatever was in the bottle wasn't what had been prescribed. Must be something they got on the street."

Emma nodded. She turned to Dick. "You still don't think that code you had last week was an overdose?"

"Which one? You can't swing a dead cat without hitting a code these days. Who knows what they're injecting."

"Mine wasn't injected, it was pills."

Dick shrugged. "Pills, popping, smoking, whatever. One way or another they'll find a way to get high, and it'll get them in trouble."

He doesn't care.

She remembered Taylor's dead friend Mike, and Taylor herself who may or may not be using. Her heart sank.

"I'm wondering if it's fentanyl," Sal said.

Dick gave him a side glance. "Fentanyl? Why fentanyl?"

"It's one of the few drugs potent enough to be almost Narcan resistant. Morphine, heroin, hydrocodone, oxycodone—they all should respond to Narcan. Even methadone."

"To various degrees," Dick agreed, "but carfentanyl and remyfentanyl don't."

"They're both so rare that we don't even have them in the pharmacy yet. And I haven't heard about either of them on the street!"

Dick shrugged. "It's just a matter of time. They're on their way, I bet. The druggies will find a way to get them. They'd do anything for a good high. That keeps us all in business, eh? Job security." He smiled, finished his drink, and turned to Kayla. "Would you like a ride?"

"Kelly'll take me."

Good for her.

12

THE TALK with Taylor didn't go well.

Nestled between the sofa cushions, her dark hair with new green ends falling across her face, she kept her eyes glued to her phone.

"Put the phone down, Taylor," Emma said.

Taylor ignored her.

"We're trying to speak to you, sweetheart," Victor said, "please."

"What?" Taylor glanced at Victor.

He opened his mouth to speak. No sound came out. He looked at Emma for help.

"We heard about Mike," Emma said, "I'm so sorry. Was he a good friend to you?"

"What did you hear?"

"He overdosed."

"What's it to you? Why do you care?"

Emma bit her lip. "Of course, I care. I'm your mother. I love you. I'm worried about you!"

"Whatever." Taylor went back to her phone.

"What's that supposed to mean?"

Emma dug her nails into her palms to refrain from grabbing Taylor's phone and smashing it against the wall.

"You don't have time for me. You're never home. Shifts, meetings, conferences, always something. You say you love me, but you don't care where I am and you don't know what I do. Your career is more important than me. Your patients are more important than me. You pay the bills and stock the fridge. That's all the attention I get. You don't even know who my friends are. And you expect me to believe that you care about Mike? Please!" Taylor rolled her eyes.

Emma swallowed the lump in her throat. *I never thought she wanted me around. She always acts like she wants to be left alone.*

Victor cleared his voice. "Taylor, we both love you. We care about you. We're worried about you."

"Well, don't be. I'm doing just fine."

"No, you're not. You're skipping school, you're failing subjects, and you have friends using drugs. That's anything but fine," Emma said.

"That's all you care about. School. You don't care about what I want, how I feel, how unhappy I am. You care about nothing but my grades."

"Bullshit! I care about everything. I care about your feelings, but school is important. It's the only way you can succeed in life and have a career."

"I don't want a career. Look at yourself. You have a career. What good does it do you?"

"Well, for one, it helps pay your bills. It pays for that phone that you can't put down and for your clothes and for your vacations!"

"Money, that's all you care about."

"No, it's not. And you don't seem to despise money quite that much when you use it, do you?"

Emma knew better than to taunt her, but she just couldn't help herself. Her blood was boiling; her breath was coming out in short angry bursts. Even worse, she was feeling guilty, because deep inside she knew that Taylor was right.

In Emma's life, everything had always played second fiddle to her career—her marriage, her pregnancy, Taylor herself. She had scheduled everything around her work. Yes, Taylor was important to her and she loved her—*I have to, I'm her mother*—but *my career, that's really important*. Not only for the money, but to silence the voice inside her that told her that she wasn't worth much, and she'd never amount to anything.

Unless I'm successful, I'm disposable. "Nobody's gonna care about you if you don't succeed," her mother said. "People only care about you if you're young and pretty, or you're rich. When you get old, they'll forget you even exist."

Emma grew up hearing that. In that deepest corner of her heart, she knew that she was disposable. *That's what happened with Victor when Amber came along. He left without looking back. As for Taylor, I could die and be buried before she'd care. To her, I'm nothing but an inconvenience.* Still, it was painfully true that she had dedicated herself to her career. In Emma's struggle to become successful, Taylor got ignored.

Victor intervened. "Taylor, what happened to Mike?"

Taylor shrugged. "He died."

"How?"

"You know how."

"What was he using?"

"What difference does it make?"

"I am... we're worried about you. Are you using?"

Taylor looked him in the eye. "So that's the problem?

You're worried that I'm an addict and that I'll OD too?" She turned to her mother. "And you? You'd be happy to get rid of me, wouldn't you!"

Emma wanted to slap her, hard.

She took a deep breath instead and stuck her fists in the pockets of her faded scrubs. "You are my child. You are my responsibility. I'll do whatever I can to protect you."

"Except for putting me ahead of your precious career, of course."

"My career is rewarding to me. It gets me money, respect, gratitude, and even love. What do I get from you besides impertinence, dirty dishes, and humiliating meetings with counselors? What do you contribute to this relationship?"

Victor intervened. "Stop that, both of you!" He turned to Taylor. "Taylor, we love you. We're worried about you. We want to help!"

Taylor shrugged. "Well, if you really want to know, Mike's overdose was not an accident. He got bullied in school. He was gay. His mother was an intolerant religious bitch. His stepfather abused him. He couldn't take it anymore. He took his mother's pain pills and went to sleep."

The silence fell, heavy.

"How come you know all that? Victor asked.

"He texted me to ask for help. I didn't get the text until it was too late. Thanks to you," she said, turning around to face Emma, her eyes daggers. "Remember that day last week you grounded me and took away my phone? He'd be alive if it weren't for you!"

Now that's my fault too! Is there anything that's not my fault? Ever?

"You know damn well why you were grounded. You didn't show up until past midnight, though your curfew was ten. You didn't even bother to call and tell me you'd be late. I spent hours sick with worry about you."

"Tell that to Mike. Is there anything else, or are we finished here?"

Helpless, Emma and Victor looked at each other.

"What do you want, Taylor? What is it that you're looking for?" Victor asked.

"I want to move out."

"Out where?"

"I don't want to live here anymore. I want to feel like a person, like I matter and somebody cares about me."

"We both care about you," Emma said, shrinking with the pain of rejection. She knew that Taylor didn't like her, but that hate? That was news.

Taylor's stare would have wilted a cactus.

"Where would you live if not here? Who'd do your laundry and your shopping and..."

"And wipe my ass," Taylor sniggered. "I can do my own shopping and my own damn laundry!"

"Really? You haven't yet shown any signs of that!"

"Emma, that's not helpful!" Victor said.

"I could go live with Katie. Her mother said it would be OK."

Katie had been Taylor's best friend since kindergarten. She lived with her mother in a trailer park south of town. Rumor had it that men would stop by every now and then, and stay for a night or for a week.

"Absolutely not," Emma said, "you aren't going to live in a trailer."

"Really? And how exactly are you going to stop me?"

Victor intervened. "How about coming to live with us?" he asked.

Taylor gave him a long, searching look. "What will Amber say?"

"She'll say, 'Welcome, Taylor.' The girls would love to have you."

The girls, Opal and Iris, loved their big sister.

"Shouldn't you talk to Amber first?"

Emma wasn't happy, but she didn't have a better plan. After all, Victor was Taylor's father, and Amber was OK. *It may do her good to live in a real family.*

"I will," Victor said. "Gather your stuff; I'll be here to pick you up tomorrow.

Taylor grinned, and Emma realized that she'd played them. Again. *That's been her plan all along, to move in with Victor. She's borderline, brilliant, and a pain in the ass. Let Victor have a taste of living with her. It serves him right.*

Deep inside, her heart was crying.

SPIDER

I'm here. It's almost nine. It's cold. Snowing. The snow's covering me. It's soft, white, and quiet.
Like a shroud.
I wait.
I wait some more.
A man comes out. Looks like him. He walks to the far parking lot, checking his phone. Fool!
Take whatever, as long as he's dead, he said.
I want the phone; maybe a laptop, his bag's heavy enough to make him slump. That would pay good.
I've got his picture, but I don't need it. I know what he looks like, but for the hood.
He gets close to the car. I check the number. It's the right car, a Mercedes, the right plate.
He opens the driver's door. I'm right behind him now, but he doesn't know. He's on the phone.
"On my way, dear, I'll be home in half an hour."
No, you won't.
I grab the knife.
The handle feels warm.

Warm and smooth.

I know what to do.

"Bring your right arm up, blade horizontal, to neck height. Grab his hair with your left and pull it sideways, the head with it. Slide the blade across his neck like the bow on a violin, waiting for the sound. It sounds like a wisp of wind inside a storm," he said, "no louder. There'll be no screaming. There's no air to go to the mouth and make sounds; after you cut the windpipe, it's all over. Soft and quiet like the wind in a forest."

"Don't leave anything behind; they'll find you if you do. Don't touch anything but him."

I'm half a step behind him as he puts his phone away to open the door.

I cough. His head whips back.

"I've got a message." The knife hangs along my thigh, out of sight. My left hand is ready.

He looks me up and down. Doesn't know me.

"What message?"

I smile and show him my empty left hand. "This," I say. He cranes his head to see.

I grab a handful of white hair and pull it back to straighten his neck. I move behind him and lift the knife to play the death song across his neck. It slides through skin and flesh like butter. His knees soften. He grows heavy.

The whisper of a scream comes out, then there's nothing but wind. Wind and blood, warm and salty in my mouth and in my eyes and all over me. I haven't been this warm in weeks!

I let him melt into the ground, softly. What if I take the car? It's a nice car, better than any I've ever had!

I know better. I pull him up. He's breathing red bubbles through the hole in his neck. His wide eyes are asking why. I don't answer. He's dead already; he shouldn't care now, should he? Dead people

don't care. I lift him into the car. He's heavy. I push his feet inside and bend his knees to close the door. I slam it shut with the hip. They'll find him, but it's gonna be a while, maybe days, before they wonder what that car is doing sitting here. The snow is falling, soft and thick and white, covering the blood, the car, now his coffin, covering me. His blood, all over me, has gotten cold. I grab his bag—mine now, and leave, walking slowly. Ten steps later I think: I should have checked for a wallet. Maybe it's in the bag. I can't go back. But maybe... No. I can't go back. I walk slowly, whistling "We Are the Champions" *to myself. I'm alone in the dark. I'm done. He's done.*
We did good.

13

EMMA CHECKED FOR HER PHONE, her glasses, her ID. All there. Her bag was empty but for her always-there gear: scalpel, flashlight, gloves, tourniquet, stethoscope. No lunch. There'd been no time for that.

The phone rang as she helped Taylor pack. As usual, Taylor wasn't talking. Emma was glad. *The only thing I'd like to tell her is this: Please, please, don't become your grandmother. And that, I can't.*

Emma was eight when she realized that she hated her mother. The woman had been mentally ill, sadistic and evil. Mother —never Mom—had spent months and months in hospitals. She was depressed, anxious, constipated. She couldn't sleep. She was always in pain. She needed constant attention, love, and reassurance. She needed more than eight-year-old Emma could provide. When denied, she started with the shaming: "One day I'll kill myself and you'll be sorry. You'll see how life is without me." The beatings came later. They were well planned and thorough. Mother would get her naked, then beat her with a stick, avoiding her hands and face, until she kneeled, asking for forgiveness, or peed herself. Preferably both. *No wonder I'm a lousy mother. I never learned better. Taylor is just like her. Manipulative, moody, self-centered. She's Mother in a younger package. Mothers are supposed to love their children unconditionally. I love Taylor, I have to, but as for liking her...*

The phone rang. The COO needed her.

"Now."

"Now?"

"Now."

This can't be good. She brushed her teeth, threw on some clean scrubs, and got her work bag. She said good-bye to Taylor and tried to hug her, but she got the "don't touch me" look.

Half an hour later she walked into the conference room, still wondering. *What the hell is this about? A patient complaint? That's Ken's job. A legal issue? A bomb threat? Are they firing me? Whatever it is, I wish they'd waited until three when my shift starts, so I could get some lunch. This is going to be a hell of a long day on an empty stomach. Unless they fire me. Then I could go have a nice dinner.* She stepped in the conference room. It was packed.

Mr. Lockhart, the CEO, sat at one end of the long oval table. His face, sharp and unsmiling, and the artificial lights reflecting off his bald scalp made him look like a mannequin in a men's store. A dejected Kurt was sitting at the other end. His sharp suit looked slept in, his face was no better. He glared at Emma with bloodshot eyes, then went back to watching his fingers. Between them were the hospital lawyer, the risk manager, and a couple of suits she didn't know. The tension in the room was thick enough to cut with a knife.

Emma found an empty seat and braced herself.

"Thank you for joining us, Dr. Steele. We've been waiting for you."

She heard the implied reprimand. She almost apologized. Almost.

Asshole. It took me less than an hour to get here. I dropped everything. I left Taylor to look after herself. Again. He can stuff it if he doesn't like it.

"I'm afraid I have bad news for you," Mr. Lockhart said.

No kidding. I thought you called me here just to thank me for my outstanding work. What am I going to do if they fire me? First, go have a nice dinner. Then think about where I'd like to live. There are plenty of jobs for ER docs everywhere. I could go to Colorado or Alaska. Or Australia. Or Guam. I wonder what the weather is like in Guam. And the food. Spicy, I hope.

"Dr. Leep died last night."

"Who?"

"Dr. Leep. Ken. He died last night."

Ken died. Her friend. Her mentor. Her Dumbledore.

"How?"

"He was found in his car with his throat cut. Police are investigating. A suicide has not been discounted."

"Suicide? Ken, cutting his throat in his car? You must be kidding!"

Lockhart shrugged. "Police are working on it."

"When did it happen?"

"He was found yesterday. Sorry, honey, I know he was your friend. He was a good doctor and a good man. Our hospital will never be the same without him."

Emma looked at Kurt. He'd been even closer to Ken than she was. "I'm so sorry, Kurt."

Kurt didn't look up.

"We'll get in touch with his wife and try to help." Mr. Lockhart continued, "However, the reason we needed to talk to you today is another but related matter. Since Dr. Leep is no longer with us, we need to establish a new ED leadership. That department needs a strong leader." He started pacing with slow, important steps. "Our community hospital has been struggling. We've been having financial difficulties. We've been in the red for the last three years. The ER is a part of the problem. I tried to address this issue with Dr. Leep multiple times. Unfortunately, we were unable to find a solution. We were forced to look at other alternatives."

Emma looked at him with narrowed eyes. *You were going to get rid of him, and he knew it. When Ken offered me the assistant director position, he knew he was on his way out. Still, he planned to retire and enjoy life. Now he's dead. What a cruel irony!*

"Since we couldn't find a solution, we looked into outsourcing our ED services. We approached EMSA, Emergency Medicine Services Association. We'd agreed to start in April, but Dr. Leep's death has brought a new urgency to this matter. EMSA has graciously agreed to start next month. This is Dr. Drom from EMSA," Mr. Lockhart said, pointing to a slim man smiling like a hungry rattlesnake on the prowl. "Are you familiar with EMSA?"

Emma shook her head.

"We are a contract group providing emergency medicine services," Dr. Drom said, smiling again as if his lunch was passing by, and it finally clicked. *We're getting fired.*

Like all the others, she'd always been a hospital employee, but the healthcare industry was changing. Hospitals started outsourcing their ERs to contract groups. That simplified their operations and helped their bottom line. Great news for the hospitals, but a disaster for the emergency docs. They lost their jobs overnight. *Hard to believe* that this can happen here, in the middle of nowhere, but it just did.

"EMSA has offered to employ all our existing physicians. They're hoping to continue the excellence of care we are known for," Mr. Lockhart said.

Kurt's jaw twitched. The engorged vein appeared like a blue worm on his left temple, looking ready to pop.

Dr. Drom smiled again. Emma wished he'd refrain. *He looks like a snake greeting a rabbit. Delighted and hungry.*

"We're happy to be here," he said. "We've heard good things about the care you folks provide to your little community. We're dedicated to continue good care, albeit in a more efficient and cost-effective manner. We hope to start a successful cooperation. We can work together toward our common goals."

"Such an excellent opportunity to revamp our care," Mr. Lockhart said. "Together we can provide the safest and most cost-effective care for the good of our community."

Emma looked from one to the other, listening to their well-practiced, cardboard speeches and wondered why she was here. *Ken is dead; Kurt was his assistant, but me? I'm just one of the ER docs.*

"We've heard about you, Dr. Steele," Dr. Drom said, looking in her general direction though not exactly in her eyes. *The little patch of hair below his lower lip looks like a hungry leech.* "You came highly recommended by some of my friends. I was really impressed with your CV."

"Thank you," she said. Kurt looked at her as if he were ready to cut her throat.

"We'd like to offer you the position of chief of the Emergency Department."

Really? They're going to ditch Kurt, like Ken said. They want me to take over. Why?

"We've already discussed that with Dr. Crump. He agrees that you will make an excellent director."

Kurt turned dark red. He swallowed. He didn't choke.

"You're too kind. Since you've seen my CV, you must know that I have no administrative experience."

"That's a positive. We'll train you. We'll get you all the help you need."

"What exactly would the job entail?"

"We will talk about that. In a moment."

Mr. Lockhart stood. The meeting was over. "We're heartbroken about Dr. Leep's demise. We'll find an appropriate way to recognize his service. Dr. Crump, thank you for your dedication and for the many years you spent caring for our patients. Tomorrow, we'll send out a memo to the ER staff outlining the things we discussed. The EMSA representatives will be available in the ED to talk to the physicians. We're happy to share the wonderful news. Nobody will lose their job!"

Kurt glared at Emma once more. He left, crumpled and hunched, a shadow of his carefully tended self.

Emma sat waiting for Dr. Drom to speak.

He didn't. He shuffled his papers and looked at her, smiling again.

She couldn't take it any more.

"Why me?"

Dr. Drom had trouble swallowing. The leech moved.

Straight talk's not his thing.

"You're young, dynamic, and unrelated to the previous administration. You were recommended to me by people I trust. You're smart enough to appreciate this extraordinary opportunity. You're a woman. Women are more flexible. They adjust better. They're also more relationship-oriented. I find that essential to making our cooperation a success."

He shuffled his papers again. "We'd like to keep the doctors, all of them,"

"Dr. Crump?"

"Him too. It would be easier for you if he left, though. He won't take kindly to your leadership."

"What are my responsibilities?"

"80 percent clinical; 20 percent administrative. Quality control, staff scheduling, new process implementation, training, recruiting, ongoing evaluation for the staff, interactive meetings with other departments..."

Emma's head was spinning.

"We'll discuss the details. We'll provide you with all the tools you need. Your success is our success."

Her brain spinning, she walked to the ED, torn between feeling heartbroken about Ken's death and being excited about the job offer. Ken had advised her against it. But Ken was dead. Very dead.

What a horrendous death! Suicide? That's ridiculous! Who would want to hurt Ken, the nicest, kindest doctor I've ever met? It makes no sense!

*S*he punched the ED code, and she remembered Taylor. *She must have left by now. Too late to call her. Room 3 is screaming in pain. The blood-covered woman in Hallway 4 looks like she's been waiting for hours. The whole place is a zoo. I'll call her later.*

She went straight to Room 3. The lanky teenager on the stretcher was still wearing his dirty blue football jersey. Lying on his side, his half-bent left leg resting on a pillow, he was screaming, staring at the lump outside his knee. His wide-eyed teammates stared in horror, standing as far away as they could.

"What happened?" Emma asked.

He ignored her.

"He was playing football and his knee got hit. He won't let me put in an IV," George said.

"No need." Emma looked the kid in the eye. "I'm sorry, this is going to hurt, but it will get better in a moment." She cupped his left heel in her left hand. She pulled the foot down, straightening the knee. Her right thumb pushed the dislocated kneecap back on top of the knee, where it belonged, almost too fast to see.

The patella fell back into place with a soft thunk. The kid stopped screaming.

"Love you, Dr. Steele," George said, smiling, the gold tooth he'd gotten in Vietnam sparkling under his brushy mustache.

"Love you too, George."

Fixing people is fun! Better than an orgasm! Maybe? It's been too long to be sure.

14

TAYLOR WAS ready to have a conniption fit. Except with nobody watching, what's the point? Her mother had left. Her father was late. Taylor was drowning in belongings. She had already filled three suitcases, but more stuff was streaming out of every drawer, closet, and shelf.

It's like the aftermath of a tornado. Clothes, books, makeup. So much stuff! What do I do with it? I didn't know there'd be so much! Her shoulders slumped. She looked at her beloved aqua seascape with seahorses and starfish. Her eyes stung. She'd opened her eyes to them every morning for years. She was deserting them now. The orange seagrass lamp was a souvenir from the Red Sea snorkeling trip when they were still a family.

That had been their last vacation together. She'd loved every moment of it. She petted the curious striped fish taking bread from her hands. She learned the new exotic tastes of tabouleh and tahini. She inhaled the scent of coffee and the heavy sweet perfumes as she walked through the souk, holding hands with her father. She tasted the sweet mint tea served in tiny tumblers. She had never been happier.

They told her the morning after they came back. *I'll never forget, if I live to be a hundred. Cheerios will forever smell like heartbreak.*

"Taylor, I want you to know that we love you very much," Victor said.

Taylor smiled, eating Cheerios from her peacock blue bowl.

"That will never change, even though your mother and I are getting divorced."

Taylor's throat tightened, and she could no longer swallow. She knew what that meant. Her friend Katie's parents had gotten divorced last year. Katie's father had left home. Katie hadn't seen him since.

Cheerios taste like ashes.

"Why?" Taylor asked, tears burning down her cheeks. "Why are you leaving?"

Her dad had looked at his hands as if they had the answer. He said nothing.

"We don't get along anymore. Our lives are different. We no longer belong together," her mother said.

"It's your fault! What did you do to him?" Taylor threw herself in Victor's arms. "Please don't leave, Daddy, please don't leave me; I can't be without you," she cried.

He held her. He kissed the top of her head. "We're going to love you just as much. We're still going to be a family," he said. Stupid lies.

She didn't blame him. She knew it was her mother's fault. She must have done something to make him leave. That's when she started hating Emma.

It took years before she understood about Amber. That

didn't change anything. She blamed her mother even more, since she felt guilty. She constructed a scenario in which Emma had forced Victor into a relationship with Amber and then thrown him out. Nothing could ever change her mind.

Right now, though, she wished her mother had been there to help. She'd deal with the mountains of stuff in her easy, competent, and annoying way. *Why does she always have to be right?* As usual, her mother was busy. Her career always came first.

The doorbell rang. It was her dad. *He looks like he hasn't slept in a week!* His eyes were bloodshot behind the steel-rimmed glasses and his hair was a mess, as usual, but his hug was like coming home.

"Are you ready?"

"Not really. I don't know what to do with all this," Taylor said, pointing to the stuff.

"Don't worry about it; we'll come back and get it later. It won't fit in the car anyhow. It's going to be safe here."

He picked up the two heavy suitcases and dragged them to the door. The faulty wheel thumped with every twist, like a broken heartbeat. He opened the back of the station wagon. He strained to lift the suitcases in.

Taylor brought out the last one. She looked back at the house. Dark red and angry, the house looked back. That was the only home she could remember, and they'd never gotten along. She slammed the door shut. She locked it. She considered throwing away the key; then she remembered all her stuff. She slipped the key in her pocket. She dragged the last bag down the steps.

Her father drove the same blue Subaru he had been driving when he left them, nine years ago. The same but for the new dent in the passenger door.

"You need a new car. Nobody believes that you're a cardiologist when they see your ride," Taylor said.

"So what?"

"You aren't cool."

He shrugged. He didn't care. He squeezed the third suitcase in with the first two, then slammed the door shut. "Hop in."

"Other kids have cool parents," Taylor said, putting on her seat belt. She examined his old muddy boots and his padded green jacket. The right sleeve was still missing the piece Thelma had eaten last year when he'd left her in the car.

"Lucky them." He started the car and looked at her. "Got everything that matters? School books, gym equipment, cell phone, purse?"

Taylor shrugged.

He shrugged back and started. His home was a good hour's drive from Emma's, on the other side of town. They worked at the same hospital, commuting from opposite directions. He skipped the downtown to take the side roads. The traffic was light. The roads were dry and white with salt. Taylor watched the patches of bright snow left on the tree branches, the hairy horses dressed in winter coats, the smoke coming out of chimneys. She wondered what dinner was going to be. Amber's cooking...

Her father cleared his voice. "Taylor, I need you to be nice to Amber."

"I'm always nice to Amber."

"Yes, but that's when you're visiting. Now that you'll live with us, the rules are about to change. Amber has a lot on her hands, with the house, the girls, and her job. I need you to be polite and help her. You shouldn't expect her to do things for you like your mother does. Did."

"Why, she started bitching already?" Taylor blurted.

Her father gave her a wilting look.

"Be respectful and polite."

Taylor swallowed her next remark.

"It would be nice if you'd help with things around the house. Cleaning the kitchen, taking the dogs out, cleaning the cat box. That would go a long way to make you appreciated." His voice was strained.

Has Amber given him a hard time?

She used to like Amber. Way more than she ever liked her mother. Amber was young and fun when they met. She was still dating Victor. Amber loved doing the girly things that Emma never did, like doing their nails and their hair. Going shopping. Their first vacation was New York City. They had a blast, eating out, shopping, going to shows. Amber was so much fun!

Then the girls came, first Opal, then Iris. Amber lost her spunk. She no longer had time to just "be girls" with Taylor. *Is this what happens when you have kids? You get to be boring and dull? I don't want kids! Ever!*

They drove up Victor's driveway, lined with Christmas trees of all different sizes—Amber was into the green stuff. They got a live Christmas tree every year, and they planted it afterward. That was nice, but their trees were always small —the roots had to fit in a container. Taylor remembered the fried tofu Christmas dinners. The morning yoga.

I wonder if leaving home was such a great idea.

The red door opened. The girls ran out to meet them. They jumped on Taylor, who picked them both up, hugging them tight. Amber, her ripped skinny jeans topped by a soft rose cashmere sweater like the one on the cover of *Vogue*, stepped out to meet them. She looked at Victor carrying the suitcases. She saw Taylor holding hands with the girls. She smiled. Her makeup was perfect, and her blonde hair fell to her shoulders like golden silk, but her smile didn't reach her eyes.

"Come in, everybody. It's cold outside."

15

KURT WAS HOLDING PRESSURE. His gloved finger had been stuck inside the bleeding gash for ten minutes now. The patient was covered in blood. So was he. Room 5 looked like the massacre scene from a cheap horror movie.

Kurt couldn't get the bleeding to stop. The thick, sticky blood had pooled in the depth of the wound. It was impossible to find the bleeder and cauterize it. He lifted his finger from the pumper, trying to see what he was doing. Warm blood, not his own, splattered his glasses, his mask, and everything else in the room.

He's got to be on something else besides Coumadin, the old rat-poison crap. It's got to be something more. Aspirin or Plavix or some freaking NOAC, the goddamn new blood thinners advertised all over TV! What the hell's happening in his brain if his scalp looks like this? He should have gone to the CT already, but he's bleeding like stink. I could throw in a couple of staples. That would stop it in a pinch, but the metal would cause so much artifact that the radiologist wouldn't be able to read the damn scan! Clinical correlation is advised! Bite me!

"Get me some Afrin spray and some gauze," he told Judy.

"Afrin?" Afrin, a nasal spray, was used for colds and runny noses, not for scalp lacerations.

She had a point, but he didn't have time to explain. "Afrin, on the quick."

Her lipless mouth told him that he was going to pay for this. The back of her navy T-shirt said it all: "Be nice to your nurses. We stop your doctors from accidentally killing you." *Damn ER nurses, they have no respect for doctors. It's always been like that, but it's gotten worse since Ken's death! The whole ER's gotten twitchy! Everybody is anxious, irritable, and ready to blow up. They miss Ken—God knows I miss him too—but they're also afraid that somebody's going to cut their throat. Police don't seem to give a shit! What the hell are they doing?*

He bent over the old man. The white hair was now a red helmet, dripping with blood from the four-inch gash. That's where his head had hit the nightstand.

"How did you fall? Did you pass out?"

No answer.

He doesn't have his hearing aids, of course! They never do. He shouted: "Did you pass out?"

"No."

"So how did you fall?"

"I don't know. I tripped, maybe?"

That's not good enough; I'll have to do a full syncopal workup with EKG and enzymes and the whole nine yards. We'll find nothing, as usual. That's how we practice medicine these days, thanks to the freakin' ambulance chasers. We spend money and resources to cover our asses since we're so afraid of getting sued. Common sense is no longer common.

Judy returned with the Afrin.

"Open it for me, will you?" he asked, his left hand still holding pressure inside the wound.

She did.

"Spray some in here. Even better, get some gauze and spray the Afrin on it. Soak it."

He nestled the gauze inside the wound, right on top of the bleeder.

"Get me a pressure dressing."

They bandaged the wound with an elastic dressing tight around the head and chin. They secured it with tape.

The bleeding stopped. The patient looked like a bloody mummy. Kurt didn't care. Neither did his patient.

"Let's get him into the scanner ASAP."

Kurt took off his bloody gloves, his blood-stained face mask, and his safety glasses. He put the glasses under the tap to wash them rather than smear the blood all over them. He took off his blue protective plastic coat. He was sweaty and dirty. He headed to the staff restroom to clean up.

Dick was leaning on Kayla's desk.

"Not today," she said. He smiled and touched her face. Kurt's blood boiled.

"Tomorrow, then?"

"Maybe." She smiled, taking in his strong frame and clear blue eyes.

Just like "The Most Interesting Man in the World" commercial, Kurt thought, feeling dirty, small, and very angry. He stopped in front of them.

"What are you doing here? Not working, are you?"

"I stopped by to talk to the EMSA folks. Did you talk to them yet?"

"Nope. Not yet." Kurt tightened his fists. His head was about to explode. He'd forgotten about EMSA, like he forgot about everything when he was working. The ED was an alternate world. It absorbed him and made him forget everything else. "What did they say?"

"We talked contracts. They don't offer malpractice."

"Really? I've never heard about any employer not offering malpractice."

Malpractice insurance was essential. Nobody'd ever dream of working without it. In the litigious medical environment when everybody could sue anybody for any reason, good malpractice coverage was a must.

"They'll help arrange for individual malpractice. We pay for it."

"No pension either, I guess."

"Yep. No pension, no malpractice, no health insurance, no nothing. You're on your own, baby."

"Are you going to sign up?"

"I don't think so. Even though there are attractions." Dick smiled at Kayla, and she smiled back. "I'm a rolling stone. I don't like to be tied to one place. I love new places and new people. Want to travel together, baby?" he asked Kayla, as if Kurt wasn't there. "There's a beautiful world out there."

Kayla smiled but didn't answer.

Kurt's urge to punch Dick choked him. He clenched his teeth, pushed his fists further down in his pockets, and turned away. He had nothing to say. He was married. He had nothing to offer Kayla. He could even lose his job if their relationship became public knowledge. *Fuck the "Me Too" movement and the overblown feminism. I can't afford to lose my job. But then, I can't afford to lose Kayla.*

Room 5 was empty; the patient had gone to the CT scanner.

Thank God for little mercies. Kurt went to the bathroom.

The cold water soothed his face and his burning eyes. To humor himself, he started fantasizing about killing Dick.

An insulin injection, maybe? Too tame. Sux? That would have him awake and hearing, but he'd be paralyzed, so that he couldn't breathe and he'd know he's dying. Maybe. I'd love to see the color of his blood though. Scalpel?

16

ANOTHER LONG SHIFT *without the light of day.*

It had been dark when she'd come in at seven. It was even darker now.

Emma hurried to her car, cursing the wind cutting through her flimsy scrubs. She scrutinized the shadows, thinking about Ken.

This stuff about suicide is crap. Doctors don't kill themselves like this. We know better ways. We have drugs and scalpels, and we know how to use them. We even know exactly where to shoot ourselves.

She'd often thought about that. She'd wondered how to do it. She didn't want to die, but she wanted to be in control of whatever happened to her when the time came.

Ken didn't cut his own throat. Somebody else did. That somebody may be here, now, in the shadow, waiting. Waiting for what? Why did Ken die? A personal vendetta? A crazy family member? A patient? One of the seekers that Ken had cut off from their candy? Something personal, like Kurt being demoted? Nah, that's not Kurt's style. Who then?

She wondered if she was at risk, walking alone through

the dark parking lot. She shivered, the cold going deep inside her heart. She checked her pockets for her short, heavy stethoscope. It was her weapon. She'd been practicing using it like a nunchaku. *I wish I had a gun, or at least a scalpel. That, I'm good with. Pepper spray! I'll get some tomorrow.* She shivered again and looked around once more before opening the car door.

Once inside, she took a deep, relieved breath, started the car, and drove home. Her neck ached, her scrubs felt tight, and her hands were hurting with cold. *I'm ready for this day to be over.*

The last straw had been the drug seeker who'd called her a cunt. Security had escorted him out, but her anger made her blood boil even now, hours later.

It had been his third visit this week. A broken tooth today, belly pain two days ago, back pain the day before. Each time he got an opioid prescription that he didn't need. *He'll either abuse it or sell it on the streets. It's surely easier to give in and give him what he wants, but it's just not the right thing to do.*

Hot with anger, she'd gone to confront Umber, who'd signed his last script.

He wanted none of it.

"You practice your way; I practice mine. You're not my boss. You don't tell me what to do."

"But he's been here three times this week looking for a fix. We can't keep giving him opiates. That's not good practice."

"The Joint Commission says, "If they say they have pain, they have pain."

"But go look at the Prescription Drug Monitoring database. See how many opiates scripts he's gotten over the last few months for a plethora of complaints. He's not here for pain. He's here for a fix."

"I have to look after patients and deal with a freaking endless amount of paperwork. I don't have time to check the freaking PDM."

"You're indulging his addiction instead of helping him!"

"Once again: I'm practicing the way I see fit. You have no business telling me what to do."

"But it's morally wrong to feed their addiction!"

"They are adults; they do what they choose to do. I'm not their guardian!"

"But you shouldn't be their drug peddler, either! You're a doctor!"

He looked like he was about to hit her.

"Get a life." He left.

She wanted to hit him. She took a deep breath instead and went back to her patients. Now that this damn shift was finally over, she needed to vent. She called Victor.

He was busy, getting the girls ready for bed.

"No, not that one, Opal. The pink one, your mother said." He sighed. "Sorry, Emma, what were you saying?"

"I had a miserable day. I hate the ED. I'm going to take Ken's advice and turn down the job."

"Ken's always been afraid of his own shadow. He never took any risks. You're not Ken."

"I thought you liked him!"

"Sure I did, everybody did, but he couldn't make up his mind to save his life."

"Still, he was right. He also said that I should spend more time with Taylor. I shouldn't take on a job being on call 24/7."

"Taylor's seventeen. She has no time for you. She'll be on

her own soon. She's out of your house already. Why on earth would you turn down a career opportunity you may never get again? You don't have to do it forever if it's not your thing."

"But I have no experience!"

"You won't get any unless you take the job."

"What if I fail miserably?"

"You won't. If you fail, you'll fail gloriously, like you always do. You'll get up and move on. It may even be good for Taylor to see you take chances and reach beyond your level of comfort," he said.

"No, not there, Iris, the other drawer. The left. The other left. Sorry about that, Emma. That ED needs some changes. I know you guys are all bent out of shape that EMSA is taking over, but that place is out of control. Everybody does whatever the hell they want. It's an absolute mess. It's high time that somebody with balls got it together, and you've got more balls than anyone I've ever met."

Emma felt warm inside. His vote of confidence was exactly what she needed. She remembered Umber: "You're not my boss; you don't tell me what to do."

"What if they backstab me?"

"They will. They backstab each other all the time; they'll backstab you even more. So what? You'll just do your job. Pay no attention to the naysayers. They'll get over it, or they'll get out."

Victor's right. I should give it a try. I can make the ED better for the patients and even the staff. I'd get to tell Umber and Crump what to do. Wouldn't that be fun!

"Thank you, Victor. I'll do it."

"Atta girl. Go get them," he said, and she could hear the smile in his voice.

17

EMMA'S PHONE RANG. They needed her back. Already.

She'd been the ED director for almost an hour, and her new job was starting off with a bang. One of her nurses was in a coma. Police were on their way.

On her way back, she thought about Ken. It had been a week. There was no progress. None that the ED folks knew of, at least. The whole place was quivering with anxiety. The staff were afraid to walk to their cars. They asked Security to chaperone them after dark. During daylight, they'd wait for each other and leave in pairs rather than risk walking alone through the parking lot. *And now this. Whatever this is.*

It was George. They'd found him unconscious in the shower room.

Police gave her a heavy stare and checked her ID before letting her in.

"You know him well?" the heavyset policewoman asked her.

"Very well."

"How long has he worked here?"

"Longer than I have. Now, if you'll excuse me..." Emma tried to walk past her into Trauma 3.

"What was he using?"

"Excuse me?"

"What drugs was he using?"

"What makes you think that he was using any?"

"Didn't they tell you?"

"Tell me what?"

"They found him with a needle in his arm."

Emma bit her tongue. She blinked. She'd thought that George had slipped in the showers, then fallen and hit his head. Or that he'd been attacked. *Apparently not.*

"I see. Who found him?"

"A nurse coming in for his shift."

"I see."

She took in the ED. *What a mess! George is in a coma after using drugs at work. Carlos, who found him, is talking to the police instead of taking care of patients. We're starting two nurses down. Everyone else is either in shock or gossiping in the corners. Nobody's looking after patients. Police everywhere, inside and out. We may as well be in shutdown.*

"Excuse me. I need to go."

The policeman guarding Trauma 3 tried to stop her, but she flashed her new ED DIRECTOR badge and pushed through.

George was lying on the stretcher. His head looked twice its size, wrapped in bloody compression bandages. A stiff C-collar stabilized his neck. He was intubated. The plastic tube connecting him to the ventilator was stuck to his face with tape crossing over his mustache. *That's going to be a bitch to remove.* She checked his vitals: Blood pressure 157/98, HR 86, O2 sat 100 percent, temperature 98.6. Judy, his nurse, was working on a third IV. Nora was doing an EKG.

"How is he?"

Judy shrugged without making eye contact. The red flash in the catheter told her that she got into the vein. She slid the needle all the way in with a smooth move and secured the IV. Safe now, she glanced at Emma.

"We're just back from CT. They said it's a brain bleed. He hasn't been conscious since we found him."

"Who's his doctor?"

"Umber."

"Has he called his family yet?"

"No. The police want to secure his home first."

Emma walked to the head of the stretcher. She squeezed George's shoulder. "I'm here, George, my friend. We'll take care of you."

He didn't move.

She went to look for Umber. She had to circle the ED twice before she found him. For once, Umber didn't look his usual cool self.

Wrinkled white coat; messed up hair; stained scrubs. Blood? Coffee? Worse?

He looked at her with bloodshot eyes.

"How is he?" she asked.

"Bad." He logged in the computer and opened George's head CT. The brain, a gray walnut inside its skull, was marred on the right by a blinding white patch. *Blood.* He was bleeding in his brain; the pressure of the blood inside the inflexible skull was squishing the soft, jelly-like brain, crushing it. The midline had left the middle, expanding, curving around the fresh blood. The right half intruded into the left by almost an inch.

Midline shift. This is the beginning of the end. The increased pressure will start pushing the brain down toward the spine, extruding it into the spinal canal.

That's the end of the end. "Awful. Just awful."

Emma imagined George's brain squeezing out of his skull with everything that made George be George. His knowledge, his sense of humor, his personality, all gone. She envisioned his dead brain liquifying, his body kept alive by the machines.

She shivered.

"I've ordered mannitol from Pharmacy to lower intracranial pressure. I talked to the neurosurgeon across the lake. I'll send him out as soon as I can get an ambulance."

"How about hypertonic saline, while you're waiting for the mannitol? We have it here."

"Yep. Any other ideas?"

"Head up at forty-five degrees. Paralyze him. Maybe even hyperventilate a little?"

"He's paralyzed already. The head up is a good idea. I'll wait to hyperventilate. I hope to get him out of here first."

Keeping the intracranial pressure low to prevent herniation was essential, but hyperventilation was risky. It reduced the blood volume, but it caused vasospasm, shrinking the blood vessels to almost nothing and cutting the oxygen supply to the brain.

That's a Hail Mary pass. What George really needs is somebody to drill a hole in his skull and drain the blood to reduce the pressure. That may give him a chance. He needs a transfer.

"Did you send a drug screen?"

"Yep. Drug screen, alcohol level, blood gas, lactate, the whole nine yards."

"How was he when they found him?"

"Agitated. He was breathing on his own, but I had to intubate and paralyze him to get him in the scanner. I panscanned him just in case, but I don't expect to find much. It's all in the head."

"Is it true that he had a needle in his vein when they found him?"

"Yes."

"Anything else?"

"A vial of propofol. Empty. Police took it."

"Ours?"

"Don't know."

Propofol, the drug famous for killing Michael Jackson, lovingly nicknamed "Milk of Amnesia" by its fans, was a white liquid sedative frequently used for procedures. *It's a wonderful drug to put patients to sleep and make them forget. Until they get too much of it and stop breathing.*

"I can't fathom why people use propofol," Emma said.

"Neither can I, but I've seen it before."

"At work?"

"Yes. A while ago, a nurse in Concord, New Hampshire. They found her blue. She'd given herself too much."

"Did she make it?"

"No."

"The crew's here," Judy said.

"Thank God. Let's get this show on the road," Umber said.

"The police don't want to let him go before they finish processing him."

"Are you kidding me? He has to go. Now." He headed to Trauma 3 where one officer was fingerprinting George while another one was inventorying the contents of his pockets. "He needs to go," Umber said.

The officer in charge stopped counting George's change. "Another thirty minutes or so and we're ready."

"He needs to go now. He doesn't have another thirty minutes."

"He's under my charge. We'll finish as fast as we can, then he can go."

"He's under my care. He goes now." Red-faced and angry, Umber leaned over the officer, ready to grab him by the throat.

Emma intervened. "One of you officers can go with him in the ambulance and continue processing him, while we are getting him the care he needs." Dick gave her a killer look. The officer glanced at her, looked apprehensively at Dick, and then nodded.

18

THE AMBULANCE LEFT. The weariness remained. This was about to be the second death in less than a week in their department, a place where they were so close that they passed around the clothes their kids had grown out of and they recycled spouses. The mood got even darker when George's wife, Mary, arrived, shrunk with pain, her wrinkled face a mask of grief.

Emma hugged her, holding her tiny frail body close, trying to squeeze away her pain.

"Where is he?"

"He's gone to the trauma center. He'll need surgery. We sent him off as fast as we could."

"They said he was doing drugs," Mary said, blowing her nose, "but that's a lie. He hasn't done any drugs since Vietnam except for pot."

"Are you sure?"

"Of course, I'm sure. I've been with him for twenty-three years. He drinks, he smokes, he does pot, and he's a pain in the ass, but he don't do no drugs."

"What if he does them but he didn't tell you?"

"He doesn't need to tell me. I know it when he's had one glass too many; wouldn't I know it when he's high?"

They had found him in the act. Unless it was a setup... But why? And who? Is she trying to protect him? But he's so sick, why would she bother to lie? "Did you tell the police?"

"Sure I did. They don't believe me. They've made up their mind. They're at home now, ripping the place apart, looking for God knows what. I told them there's nothing to find, but they wouldn't listen."

"Mary, if he's been doing drugs, who would know?"

"He isn't."

"If he was, who would know?"

"Listen to me, he isn't. He doesn't have money for cigarettes unless I give it to him. We can't afford to fill the tank; we only get twenty dollars' worth of gas at a time. Where do you think he'd get money for drugs? Santa?"

"What if he stole drugs from here? He could get them for free. It's easy. If the doctor ordered a dose of Dilaudid, George could just use it himself and give the patient some saline. He'd come back and say that the patient needed more. The doctor would order another dose. It would be even easier if the drug was ordered PRN—as needed. He could give it as often as the patient complained of pain. One for the patient, one for himself—nobody would ever know."

"I don't believe it."

"What do you think then?"

"Somebody tried to get rid of him."

"Who? And why?"

"I don't know. But what I do know is that my George doesn't do drugs. Now I'm going to see how he is."

"Let me get somebody to drive you."

"I'll drive her," the policewoman said. Her knowing eyes looked at Mary with pity.

SPIDER

I'm back.
I got my fix, but it's over. I'm out again.
I sold the phone. Finished that money too.
I need more.
He's got it.
He's gonna give me some more.
He's one of the white coats. I just don't know which one.
I know his voice. "If you cut all the way through the windpipe, he won't scream," he said.
I'll find him.
I sit and wait.
They won't know me. I got rid of my old coat.
This one's pink, but it's got a hood and it's warm.
I wait. A white coat comes out.
"Got a cigarette?"
He says, "No."
Not him.
I try the next one.
And the next one.

19

It was past midnight when Emma finally made it home. She pushed the deadbolt, dropped her bag, and picked up a bottle of red. A Chilean Carménère tonight, an in-your-face wine with much body and little subtlety, so dark one couldn't see the light pass through, unlike those weakling pinots from Washington State, so soft-spoken they looked watered down.

This wine reminded her of Dick Umber. No subtlety about him, no compromise, no softness. As she took her first sip, filling her mouth with the dry, tannin-laden strength, chewing it to bring its flavor under the tongue and behind the teeth to strike every taste bud, she wondered if she liked Dick. She wasn't sure. He was a good doctor, but he was too macho and too much of a showoff.

He could be charming when he chose to be, like with Kayla. That side of him was reserved for pretty girls and important people. She took another sip and remembered that she was the new Ken, therefore important in Dick's world. In the ED world, in fact. Ken was right; everything that happened was her problem. And there was a lot.

Ken's death, to start with. The police had finally concluded that it wasn't a suicide, but there was no further progress.

His death and the attack on George must be related; it's too much of a coincidence to have them both happen here in less than a week.

She had started going around asking questions. She got some answers. Judy remembered a funny little homeless man asking about Ken one night when she was working in triage. He had a gift for Ken, he said. He wanted to thank him for taking care of his son. *That's unusual. Grateful patients may bring some cookies or donuts, but gifts are rare, especially from somebody who looks like he can't afford a cup of coffee.*

"What was he like?" Emma asked.

"Homeless. Disheveled. Bad teeth."

"Anything else?"

"He had a long gray coat with a badge. Like a military something. He dragged his left leg."

Judy's face lit up as she remembered: "He had a spider tattoo on his right hand. Like the whole hand was a spider and the fingers were its legs. Gross!"

This is something. Maybe. I'll talk to the other triage nurses and the security people tomorrow.

She drank down her wine and headed to Taylor's room to check on her. The room was a mess, as usual. It took her a moment to remember that Taylor was gone, and she was half ashamed and half relieved. She thought about Victor. He had Taylor and Amber, both. Lucky him! She poured herself another glass, wondering how Taylor was doing.

She sat on her crumpled bed looking at the family picture on the dresser. *How young we were! Taylor was just a baby. We were still in love.* Victor, dressed in faded scrubs, was smiling, his hair a riot of dark curls falling over his glasses. Taylor, her eye color still undefined, was sitting on his shoulders squinting at the camera. Emma, thin and pretty in her flowery dress, sporting huge dark circles around her eyes from lack of sleep, leaned into him.

Life was good.

Taylor's moods got worse when Victor left for his fellowship. *She's missing her daddy*, they thought. *It will get better soon.*

It got worse. A psychiatrist diagnosed her as bipolar. He started her on mood stabilizers. They stabilized nothing, neither her flash mood changes, nor her angry outbursts or her violent rages. She became the evil genie of the house and Emma's albatross.

Emma poured another glass of wine. She remembered Mary. And George.

All the staff is getting tested regularly. George must have been clean; otherwise he'd be gone. A setup? Why?

The phone rang. It was Ann. She was pissed. As usual. She was talking so fast that Emma could barely follow.

"What happened?"

"I need you to come in right now!"

"Why?"

"I'm tired of fighting with the hospitalists! They don't call back for hours, and then they ask for all sorts of shit before they bother to come see the patient! This has to stop!"

"What exactly happened?"

"Come here and I'll tell you!"

"Why don't you tell me first?" *I've been there the whole day; I've got another shift tomorrow—no, today now. This is just Ann being Ann—she can be a charmer, but she'd rather be a raging bitch. You never know which Ann you'll get; it depends on her meds. She needs to up her dosage.*

"I have this 69-year-old with AMS." AMS, altered mental status, could be anything from not remembering where you left your keys to being unresponsive. It made it hard to get the story, so there was a lot of work to do to rule out badness.

"The hospitalist doesn't even want to see her. 'Admit her to psychiatry,' he said."

"Does she have a psychiatric history?"

"Not that we know of."

"Is she coming from home or a nursing home?"

"She lives alone."

"What's the matter with her?"

"She's confused."

"Anything on the workup"

"Nope. Labs are OK, head CT is OK, vitals are stable. I'm waiting for the drug screen and alcohol level. She's not septic or hypercapnic."

"Does she need an LP?"

"No fever, no white count, no neck rigidity. If they really want a spinal tap, they can do it themselves."

"No neuro deficits?"

"None new."

"Who did you speak to? And what did they say?"

"I spoke to Gandhi. He said there's nothing medically wrong with her, send her home or admit her to psychiatry."

"Did he see her?"

"No. He says he's five behind and he doesn't have time for this crap."

Gandhi, the night hospitalist, was busy. Five behind, that meant five patients waiting for orders and for hospital beds, five families snapping at the nurses, and five ER beds boarding admitted patients. That was bad all around.

"He needs to see her. He has no room to talk before he's seen her."

"Yes, Director. I wish I was smart enough to think of that."

Ann's being a bitch. That's Ann's superpower. She could bitch at Gandhi and have him come see the patient, but no, she calls me instead. In twelve years I'd called Ken only once, when a bus caught on fire and we had a mass casualty incident. Calling me for this?

Still, Emma's first instinct was to help Ann and make friends. Fortunately, she knew better. *Ann doesn't need friends. She needs servants. Giving in to her would only teach her to do it again.*

"I agree. He can't refuse to admit her without seeing her and leaving a note in the chart."

"What are you going to do?"

"Me? Nothing. Ann, I know you can manage this. I have faith in you."

She hung up, smiling.

It's good to be king.

20

KAYLA WAS LATE AGAIN.

Eden was playing on the floor with Lego blocks while Clarissa was cleaning up. He looked up when he heard the door slamming. *He's been crying,* Kayla thought.

"I'm so sorry, sweetheart!" she said, kneeling on the floor next to him, forgetting the nylons and the pencil skirt riding up her thigh. She hugged him, looking over his head to Clarissa, her eyes apologizing. "I'm sorry, Clarissa, I didn't mean to..."

"You never mean to," Eden said. "You never mean to, but then you do." He stopped crying and started putting Legos away. "You forgot again?"

"No, I didn't." She stood up looking regretfully at the nylons. *Gone.* "Something came up."

"What?"

"What did you do today? Were you a good boy?"

"*He's* always good," Clarissa said.

But I'm not. Kayla wished she were a better mom. *I should get it together, but it's so hard to be a single mom, and work, and go to school. It would be nice to have a little time off once in a while and have some fun!* After all, she was only twenty-four! Except that last time had been no fun. Kurt had been in a bad mood. He didn't like Dick's interest in her. He wanted to know if she'd gone out with him, if she liked him, if she was planning to see him. As if he had a right to know!

She got pissed. "Do I ask you what you do with your wife?"

"But Kayla, you know how much I care about you!"

"I care about you too, but that's not the point. You have your life, and I have mine. We need to respect each other's privacy. I never ask what you do with Sheila. I don't see how it's any of your business what I do.

"But Sheila is my wife!"

"So?"

"You barely know Dick! He's nothing to you!"

"And that's your business how?"

"But you and I, we have a relationship! I care about you!"

"I care about you too, but my relationship with others is none of your business."

"So you do have a relationship with Dick." His shoulders slumped, the fight going out of him.

She felt sorry. She wanted to tell him no. She barely knew Dick. They'd gone out for dinner once. That was it. There was something about him... *He's slippery. He looks at every girl. They say he spent some time in a closet with the new CNA. I don't trust him.* She'd seen pictures of his boat and his vineyard, but his Facebook page was blank.

Still, none of this was Kurt's business.

He looked so crushed that she almost broke down to tell him the truth. Almost. *He wants to have his cake and eat it too; he goes back home to his wife every night.* The only weekend they'd ever spent together had been a conference in Florida, that time when Sheila couldn't make it. Kurt had taken her instead, but whenever they were in public, he'd acted as if he didn't know her. It had been humiliating. *I'm only temporary in his life. It's high time to stop waiting for him and get a life. Dick is charming, generous, and single.*

"Sorry, Kurt, that's the way it is." She had left swallowing tears, but she hadn't looked back.

Eden shook her hand.

"What?"

"Can we go to McDonald's?"

That wasn't the healthiest dinner, but she was feeling guilty... and he was so skinny... and he had been so good... and there was nothing to eat at home... "Sure, let's go."

"Wahoo!"

Kayla smiled. Happiness is easy when you're five.

Clarissa shook her head. "You're going to spoil him rotten one of these days!"

"You'll make sure it doesn't happen." Kayla hugged her. "Thank you, Clarissa, and I'm so sorry."

"S'ok. How did the exam go?"

"It went well, I think. I was done almost an hour early."

"When do you get the results?"

"Next week. If I pass, I move on."

Kayla was working on her college degree. She had two years left. She'd dropped out when she had Eden, since she couldn't juggle work and school and motherhood. Now that he'd gotten older, she had gone back. She'd already passed four of the third-year exams. Only one left. *Next year should be easier, with Eden old enough to go to school.* The one thing that got her was the lack of sleep. The other day she'd fallen asleep at her desk. Dr. Steele had woken her up gently but firmly and had brought her coffee. She'd been embarrassed and apologized, but Dr. Steele had just ruffled her hair and said, "It's OK, nobody died, kid. Just try to get more rest." *She gave me a look. I wonder if she knows about Kurt. We've been discreet, but then there was that one time in the parking lot...*

It's not easy to be working full-time and study while being a single mom, but I wouldn't change it for the world.

She unlocked the door of her new Nissan and helped Eden in.

"McDonald's it is."

21

THE WOMAN on the hallway stretcher looked more dead than alive. Her conjunctivae, the white of her eyes, was too white, her skin ash gray.

Emma glanced at her as she was passing by, then went to look her up. The chief complaint was rectal bleeding. Emma went back to speak to her. *She's having trouble answering questions. No monitor. No IV access. No good.* Emma went to Brenda, the triage nurse.

"This patient needs a room."

"There are no rooms." Brenda turned around and left.

Brenda knows better. She must be busy.

"Kayla, who's in charge?"

"Judy. Should I get her?"

"Please." *Who can come out to make room for this GI bleeder? Room 6 is waiting for her psychiatric evaluation. Being in the hallway in her blue paper scrubs isn't going to do her any good, but more importantly, Room 6 isn't monitored. Trauma 2 is empty. That should work.*

"Yes?"

"Judy, we need this patient in a room. She needs an IV and monitoring."

"What's wrong with her?"

"Rectal bleed."

"Is she actively bleeding?"

"Let's get her in a room and find out, shall we? Can't do it in the hallway."

"We don't have any rooms at the moment."

"Yes, we do. Room 2 is empty."

"Yes, but it hasn't been cleaned, and it's waiting for an ambulance bringing in a transfer."

"No, it's not. We have a sick patient in the hallway. She needs the room. We can't have that room sitting empty for whenever somebody shows up."

Judy shrugged, told Kayla to send the cleaning crew to Trauma 2, and left.

I'm getting a lot of that lately. My old friends don't like me anymore. The other day she'd asked Alex to have a look at a rash. "I've got my own patients," he huffed. Brenda and Judy were behaving like spoiled children. Ann had asked to try on Emma's new white coat. "You're obviously not counting your calories," she smirked, and her nurses laughed. Emma laughed too—what else was there to do?—but she felt hurt. *Thank God for Sal, who's still my friend.* The doctors from all the other departments—hospitalists, surgeons, radiologists —had been supportive. Even former foes had cut her some slack. *All but my own. They're trying to bring me down.*

"It's because you're a woman," Minerva said later that day when they met at the gym. "Nobody likes a powerful woman, neither the women nor the men."

"Why?"

"The men, because it's not manly to have a woman lead. The women, because it's you and not them." She wiped her sweat off, pointing to the skinny blonde on the cycle. "See her?"

"Yes."

"I'm so envious of her body that I hope she'll sprout a hernia. I'd give her one if I could. Same with your people; they are envious of your power. They'd like to see you fail, like I'd like to see that girl fat and ugly just to feel better about myself, to see myself as less old and inadequate."

"You're neither old nor inadequate!"

"Whether I am or not is irrelevant. What's relevant is how I feel. She doesn't make me feel good about myself, just like you don't make them feel good about themselves."

"What can I do?"

"Hang in there. Do your thing. Be a good doctor; be a good leader. They'll get over it."

Minerva, the eternal optimist. I hope she's right. Ken warned me. I don't know how long I can do this. There's only so much wine my liver can take.

SPIDER

I found him.

Two days I sat on the bench, asking for a light from every man with a white coat.

Security came. "What are you doing here?"

"Waiting for my girlfriend."

"Who's your girlfriend?"

I showed them a picture of Jess. Naked.

They looked away.

"She works in the kitchen. She left me. I want her back."

"You can't sit here on the bench every day."

I left.

I drove back in a motorized shopping cart I got from Walmart. It had just enough juice to get here; then it died.

They didn't say nothing. Can't bother a cripple.

This morning I found him.

"You have a light?"

He looked at me with eyes the color of water. "No."

"A cigarette?"

"Why do you need a light if you don't have a cigarette?" he laughed.

That laugh made me cold inside.

It was him.

"I don't need a light; I need a fix, boss."

He looked at me sharply.

"The fish-knife. It worked. I need another fix."

"I don't know what you're talking about."

"Sure you don't. We never met, you and me. I need a fix. Soon. Like today."

He looks at me.

"No hurry. Tonight's good. I'll be back at ten. I'll look under the bench for my fix. Maybe it's there. Maybe not. Maybe I know you. Maybe I don't."

"You sure about that?"

"No, not sure. But I kept the knife. The box. The photo. And the instructions. I'll leave them under the bench if I find my fix. If not, maybe police wants them."

"Maybe," he says.

I get off the cart to shake out the numbness. I'll be back.

22

"WHAT DO you mean you don't know where she is?" Emma blurted into her phone.

Judy turned to stare at her.

I'm too loud. She walked to the abandoned X-ray reading room and pulled the door shut to get some privacy.

"She didn't come home last night," Victor said. "I was on call and I never got home, but Amber says she hasn't seen her since yesterday. The girls haven't seen her either. I don't think she ever came home from school."

"Did you call her?"

"Five times. I texted her, too. No answer, but she could still be asleep."

Almost ten. She could be, she sleeps every Saturday till noon. But where is she?

"Did you try Katie's house?"

"I didn't. Can you?"

"I'm at work, damn it. I can't leave here till four. I'll call her, but how about if you drive over to Katie's and call me back?"

"I was supposed to take the girls skiing. Amber is going out for lunch with her friends."

"I'm sorry, but I can't leave here right now," Emma said, stepping out into the fully lit chaos outside. "Code 66, Emergency Department. Dr. Steele to Room 3."

"I have to go." She hung up and headed to Trauma 3. The paramedics were moving a wiggling, half-naked man covered in vomit onto the ER stretcher. *He's breathing.* She counted the "motherfuckers" while donning plastic gloves. She got to three. *Breathing well.*

"What's up?" she asked, grabbing his dirty boots to help move him.

"We found him unresponsive in the McDonald's parking lot," Lou said.

"On the ground?"

"No, in a truck."

"Parked?"

Lou nodded.

"Alone?"

"Yes. Driver's seat, safety belt on."

"And?"

"He had a pulse, but he was barely breathing, eight to ten a minute. His oxygen sats were in the 80s."

"Blood pressure?"

"Was OK."

"Then?"

"We gave him Narcan."

"How?"

"Intranasally."

"How much?"

"Two mg."

"Once?"

"Yes. He came to and started swearing."

That's what they do. You get them out of a high and throw them into withdrawal. That hurts. That's why it's worth being stingy with the Narcan. You want to give them just enough to get them breathing, but not enough to wake them up; otherwise, you get this. If they arrest or stop breathing though, then it's full steam ahead no matter what. They wake up, and they want to leave. Narcan wears off fast. They look OK, they take off, and then they drop dead. Bad plan.

"Where's my phone, you motherfuckers? I wanna call my lawyer! I'll sue your asses, every one of you!"

Funny how all my patients have a lawyer on speed dial. "Restraints, and security, please."

"I'm Doctor Steele; I'm glad to meet you." The patient, held down by the paramedics, made eye contact and spat at her. The phlegm came down to land on his own cheek. Emma wiped away the few drops that had reached her. "What is your name?"

"You motherfucker!" Somebody laughed.

"I doubt that. How are you feeling?" She checked his pulse, palpated his abdomen, and considered listening to his lungs. *Nope. That's getting too close.* "Let's get him a mask, and get those restraints. This week please, rather than the next."

"Let me go, you assholes. You can't keep me here. I know my rights."

"We'll let you go as soon as we know you're safe."

He exploded into another string of obscenities.

Emma was glad to see that he was breathing well, wasn't slurring his curses, and looked intact. She returned to her desk to place orders, when she remembered: Taylor was missing. She checked her phone. Two missed calls: one from Victor, one from Amber.

She stepped back in the dark reading room to call Victor.

No answer.

Tried again.

Still nothing.

She couldn't bring herself to call Amber. She didn't want to hear how Taylor was creating havoc in Amber's home and setting a bad example for her daughters. *I can't deal with that right now. How on earth can I take off to look for Taylor? The place is a zoo.*

"Kayla, can you find somebody to take over my shift?"

"This shift?"

"Yes, there's a problem with my daughter. I need to go."

Kayla picked up the phone. *Slim chance. Who'd come in on a beautiful Saturday on a minute's notice to pick up half a shift?*

Her phone rang. Amber. Emma sighed.

"Hi, Amber."

"Emma, I'm so sorry."

"Yeah, me too."

"She had breakfast with us yesterday. She looked fine. She took the bus to school, and I haven't heard from her since."

"Did she go to school yesterday?"

"I don't know. When she didn't come home yesterday afternoon, I thought she was out with her friends. We didn't worry until she didn't show up this morning. She wasn't in her room. I don't think she's been here since yesterday morning, but I'm not sure."

"Is her stuff still there?"

"There're piles of stuff everywhere, I don't know what's missing."

"Her computer?"

"She took it to school."

"Did Victor get to speak to Katie?"

"He's there now."

"Amber, do you have contact information for any of her friends besides Katie?"

"I don't."

"Can you check in her room and see if you find anything? I'm so sorry to impose on you, but I'm at work and I can't leave now."

"Sure. I'll call you back."

"Thanks."

23

SHE WENT BACK to running the board. The kid in Room 6 looked better after fluids and Motrin. His heart rate was down; he was slobbering happily, chewing on his mother's phone. *It's probably just a virus.* "Let's PO challenge him and send him home," she told Carlos. That was ED jargon for "Give the kid something to drink."

"Popsicle?"

"Whatever he'll take."

The woman with suicidal ideation in Room 7 was still drunk. At least that's what her numbers said. She needed at least another hour before being legally sober for her psychiatric evaluation. She'd been awfully drunk last night when the police brought her in. She was angry at her significant other, so she told him that she was going to jump from a bridge. He called 911.

I've heard that a thousand times, even when there's no bridge within a hundred miles. When they sober up, they deny they ever said it. They swear they'd never, ever hurt themselves because of their love for God, for their children, or for their dog, but somehow it all goes out the window after the second drink.

She ordered a repeat alcohol level, also a Tylenol and aspirin level to make sure that the woman hadn't ingested anything else.

"Dr. Steele!" Kayla called. "I found one."

Found one what?

"Dr. Alex. He's coming to take over for you. He said, 'Don't see any new patients, just clean up what you can.' He should be here in half an hour."

"Really!" Emma's eyes filled with tears, and she hugged Kayla.

"I hope she's OK."

"Me too."

When Alex arrived she was ready. "Thank you!"

"No problem. What have you got?"

"The kiddo in 6 can go if he keeps his Popsicle down. The woman in 7 needs a crisis eval."

"Can she go or does she have to stay?"

"She can go, I think. Just give her a once-over first."

"OK."

"The guy in 3, his discharge is in the chart. He can go if he's still awake in an hour. Got Narcan about an hour ago."

"No trauma?"

"Not that we know of, but walk him first."

"Anything else?"

"No. Thank you, Alex."

"No problem. Remember when you came in for me last year when I ran over my dog?"

"No."

"Well, I do."

Emma drove to Victor's house. She rang the doorbell. Thelma and Louise started barking. They'd been hers, once. When they divorced, Victor took them. Emma got Taylor. *Lucky me!*

The door opened to an avalanche of kids and dogs jumping on her and hugging her waist and legs. She hugged them all back, kissed the girls, scratched the dogs, and then turned to see Amber.

"Go play, everybody."

They took off as one.

Taylor's room looked like the aftermath of a hurricane, but the bathroom was almost empty. A white piece of plastic was sitting on the counter.

A pregnancy test.

Positive.

24

EMMA WAS WALKING SO FAST down the Administration hallway that the stethoscope was banging on her chest with every hurried step. She tried to stuff it in her white coat pocket, but with the scalpel, hemocult developer, rectal testing cards, and tongue depressors, her pockets were already full.

I really don't have time for this crap now. What on earth is so urgent that it can't wait until the end of my shift? Administrators are important people; they don't like to wait.

She shrugged as she remembered that she was now one of them, as her ER folks told her daily. Everything that didn't work right, from slow radiology reads to the Internet interruptions or the lack of Dilaudid, was her fault—or at least her problem. *This isn't half as much fun as it used to be. And of course, they're all here already, waiting. Déjà vu.*

She nodded to the sour-looking COO and sat in the only empty chair. The plump risk manager was there, so was the anorexic hospital lawyer, sitting next to a wiry man with short gray hair that she hadn't met. The policeman who'd been investigating George's case and had a pissing match with Umber was there too.

George had made little progress; he was still in the ICU, intubated. He'd had an emergency craniotomy. They removed part of his skull to allow his brain to swell without getting crushed. His prognosis was still uncertain.

Mr. Lockhart, the COO, pointed to the steel-haired man. "You already know Officer Boulos. This is Detective Zagarian. He has news for us. He requested your presence."

Why me? Taylor? It can't be; none of these people has anything to do with her. Then what?

"We received the victim's lab results," Zagarian said.

Victim? Oh, George! She'd never thought about him as a victim, not even when she'd seen him intubated.

"He had propofol in his system. A lot. We don't know how much he actually got, since we aren't sure when it was injected. There were no other drugs in his system except for cannabis."

Mary was right. He wasn't using anything but pot.

"His head injury matches the corner of the shower. What bothers me though is that he was found fallen forward, while his injury was at the back, in the occipital area."

"Maybe he turned around after he fell?" Emma asked. "Or maybe the person who found him moved him to see if he was breathing?"

"That's possible," Zagarian acquiesced, "but there's one more problem." He looked at each of them in turn as if he expected someone to confess. "He had a neck injury."

"That's not so unusual," Emma said, "depending on the way he fell he may have fractured..." She remembered: *I've seen the neck CT. There was no fracture.*

"The injury was to the front of his neck. Bruising around his Adam's apple, suggesting strangulation."

The silence in the room grew heavier.

"How old was that injury?" Emma asked. *Could he have been in another fight before?*

"Fresh. The bruising was absent in the first set of pictures, but it became obvious after the transfer, in the second set of pictures."

"So you're thinking that somebody strangled him in the shower, hit his head against the concrete corner, and then injected him with propofol?"

"Exactly. It could also be the other way 'round—someone strangled him until he passed out, then injected him with propofol, and then hit his head against the concrete. Interestingly, the propofol vial found at the scene didn't come from your pharmacy. It came from somewhere else."

"From where?" the COO asked.

"We don't know. Yet." He looked at each of them and said, "The reason I called you here today is to make it clear that we are now investigating this case as an attempted murder. We'll interview the staff. We expect you to cooperate to the extent that you can. We'll make arrangements to talk to each of you."

Lucky us. Emma stood and headed out the door before anybody could stop her, but Zagarian caught up with her. "I'll walk with you.

"We spoke to his wife. She said she has no idea why or who would want to kill him."

"I agree. I can't imagine anybody hating him that much."

"That much? Did he have enemies?"

"He liked to laugh and make fun of people. He could be a little rough."

"How did he get along with his wife?"

"Mary? As well as any couple who've been together for decades. They bickered a lot about money—money was always tight for them, especially after Mary lost her job last year—and about smoking. They both smoked, then blamed each other for not quitting. Mary was devastated when this happened, and I have absolutely no reason to suspect her."

"Could it all have happened by chance? What if George walked into the shower, found someone injecting, and they tried to silence him?"

"I guess that's possible... But you know, this isn't really the kind of place where nurses inject themselves in the shower on a daily basis."

"Well, maybe it wasn't a nurse, and it doesn't have to be daily."

Emma shrugged.

"We also considered blackmail. George's finances weren't as bad as you think. There's $10,000 in his personal checking account. Where do you think that money is coming from?"

"I have no idea." *They weren't well off, Mary and George. That money could have made a big difference, but where on earth was it coming from?*

"I have to go now, detective," Emma said, punching in the code to open the ER doors. She'd been gone for half an hour, which in ER time is an eternity—anything could have happened in that time, and it usually did.

"Thank you for your help. Remember that this is confidential; please don't discuss it with the staff."

"Really? I was just getting ready to post it on Facebook," she said, turning to leave.

He caught her elbow. She looked back. His gray eyes were smiling.

"Wanna be Facebook friends?"

Is he kidding?

"Or maybe just go for a coffee one of these days."

Is this professional or personal? He was attractive and she was single—way too single—but he was a cop.

I don't like cops.

"Maybe I'm just trying to pick your brain," he said, as if he could read her thoughts, "or maybe not. You won't know until you try, will you?"

He said until, not unless.

"Dr. Steele to Room 2," the speakers called. She was grateful for the interruption.

She left without another word.

SPIDER

I'm back.
It's half past ten. I gave him extra time.
I sit on the bench.
I bend over to tie my boot and look under.
There's a blue plastic bag. Small.
I pick it up.
A brown paper bag inside.
I open it.
A zipper bag, snack size. White powder. Like salt but lighter.
I open it. I smell it.
I taste it.
It's my fix. Good.
I close it. I put it in my pocket.
A photo. Car number on the back.
I know this one.
Keep the knife, he says.
Good.
This one's easy.
Fun too.

25

THE GRAY-HAIRED WOMAN in Room 2 gasped for air. Her bony chest, wrapped in the flimsy hospital gown, heaved with every hard-fought breath. Attached to the monitors via multiple wires, she sat upright with her face jutting forward as if she was sniffing. She held herself upright, skinny arms supporting her torso, hands clutching her knees.

Textbook tripoding. She's struggling to move air even though her oxygen sat is 100 percent. That's weird. Bad asthmatics and old smokers with bad lungs would tripod to get more oxygen, but, by the numbers, she had all the oxygen her blood could carry.

Emma went to introduce herself.

"Hi, Emma."

It took a moment.

Sheila, Kurt's wife.

They hadn't met in ages, since she and Kurt didn't socialize. She'd never seen Sheila in the pathetic disguise of a hospital gown. Still, she hadn't aged well.

"Sheila?! What happened?"

"I'm having... a hard time... breathing."

"Since when?"

"This morning... or last night..."

"Anything else? Fever, chest pain, cough?"

"No."

"Are you a smoker?"

"No."

"Any medical problems?"

"Depression... Anxiety... two miscarriages."

Emma had heard about the miscarriages; people said they had ruined the marriage.

Why on earth would people want to have children? They're nothing but trouble! She hadn't slept in days, looking for Taylor who was still MIA.

"Any allergies?"

"No."

"Have you ever had anything like this before?"

"No."

"Any rash, any tightness in your throat? Any vomiting or diarrhea?" Emma asked, wondering if this could be an allergic reaction.

"No."

Sheila was tiring out. Her oxygen sat was still 100 percent, but she was breathing fast at 40—instead of the normal 16. Her heart rate, 132, was way too high.

She's sitting still, but her body behaves like she's running a marathon.

Emma listened to the lungs—clear as a bell—and to her heart—fast, but regular with no murmurs. She checked the EKG, unremarkable except for the tachycardia, the fast heart rate. The skin was clear, blood pressure was OK, no voice change to indicate an airway problem.

"Did you try any new foods, any new medications, any

new detergents or lotions or soap, anything that your body may not be used to and might react to?"

Sheila shook her head no, but averted her eyes.

"Any alcohol or drugs?"

"No."

What on earth is going on? She looks fine, but she's breathing so hard! A PE? She has no risk factors for blood clots, and her sats are 100 percent. Anxiety? A panic attack?

"Any ringing in your ears?"

"Yes... my ears started ringing... this morning... how did you know?"

Emma turned to Faith, Sheila's nurse. "Let's give her a breathing treatment and ten milligrams of Decadron, just in case. Have you sent a blood gas?"

Faith was new. She had just moved in from New Hampshire and was still learning the ropes.

"No. It wasn't part of the protocol."

"Let's send it, please, also send Tylenol, aspirin and alcohol levels, and a urine and a drug screen. And let's get a chest X-ray, today if possible, and we'll get respiratory with bipap to give her some rest."

Faith shrugged and left.

"Sheila, did you overdose on aspirin?"

Sheila looked down. "Yes."

"How much and when?"

"Last night... I don't know, a handful... I didn't count."

"Did you take anything else?"

"No."

"Tylenol?"

"No."

"Are you sure?" Emma asked, holding her eyes, her hand on Sheila's shoulder.

"Yes."

Sheila's tears started streaming down her cheeks.

Emma hugged her. "I'm so sorry. We'll make you better."

Sheila hugged her back.

"Why aspirin?"

"They said it doesn't hurt."

It may not hurt, but it doesn't feel good either. Her body is trying to get rid of the acid in the aspirin by breathing it out. Aspirin is a killer. She may need dialysis to remove it. That requires planning and much better IV access than she's got. I'd better call them early. She's going to need a psych eval, but that can wait. Keeping her alive comes first.

"Does Kurt know?"

"He didn't... come home... last night."

"Would you like to call him?"

Sheila shook her head no.

"Would you like us to?"

Sheila started crying harder.

"Yes, please."

"Anybody else you want us to call?"

Sheila started crying even harder. "There's nobody else."

How awful, to be sick and alone. At least I'm not sick. As for alone...

She went to put in orders and checked her phone again. Still nothing from Taylor, and nothing from the police. It was getting old.

26

EMMA AND VICTOR had looked everywhere. They asked Katie. She said she didn't know. *She's lying. She's not worried about Taylor, and that's not like her. She knows.*

"Please, Katie, help us find her!"

Katie shrugged. Her old green sweater and ripped jeans made her look fragile and much younger than Taylor, but she was steady as a rock.

"You know where she is!"

Katie stayed silent.

"What if she's not safe? What if somebody's holding her against her will? We need to help her!"

No answer.

Katie's mother tried, too.

"Katie, if you know where she is, you must tell them! If you disappeared and I didn't know where to find you, I'd be sick with worry!"

They'd gone to her school. Nobody knew anything. She'd been to all her classes but the last. She didn't take the school bus home. The school counselor didn't know anything either, but she was going to ask her friends. *Her friends? I don't even know who they are, except for Katie!*

"Do you know any of her friends?" she'd asked Victor. "Other than Katie?"

"Tom."

"That's old news."

Victor shrugged. "It's all I've got."

"We didn't watch her well enough. I had tried so hard to not be like my mother, who wanted to know everything. She used to open my letters and interrogate my friends. I wanted to give Taylor more freedom. I wanted to trust her." Emma was talking to Victor, but even more, she was trying to persuade herself. *Yeah, maybe so. But, really, I was relieved when Taylor minded her own business so that I could focus on my career. I'm a lousy mother.*

"That's all water under the bridge. What do we do now?"

They went to the police.

"How long has she been missing?" the elderly detective asked.

"Since yesterday at one," Emma said.

"That's barely twenty-four hours. She may have spent the night with a friend."

"She never did that before without letting us know! We've been trying to contact her by email and text and phone. No answer."

"Maybe she doesn't want to speak to you. Did you have a fight before she left?"

"No," said Victor.

Emma shrugged. She hadn't seen her since she moved to Victor's.

"Have you tried her friends and her school?"

"Of course. Nothing."

"How about grandparents, cousins, extended family?"

Emma's parents were both dead, but Victor's mother, Margret, a lovely old lady who spent her days gardening, lived in Georgia. She was Taylor's favorite person.

"There's only my mother; we didn't want to alarm her."

"Well, you can file a missing person and we'll see what we can find. Still, you should get in touch with everybody who may have some information."

"She might be pregnant," Emma blurted; then she wished she hadn't. She hadn't had a chance to tell Victor yet.

"What?" Victor looked ready to strangle her.

"Amber found a pregnancy test in Taylor's room. It was positive."

Victor's face turned gray, and the pain in his eyes hurt to watch.

I wish I had found a kinder way to tell him. No matter what, Victor still thinks that Taylor is a little angel. This has got to hurt him even more than it hurts me!

"I'm sorry, Victor. Let's call your mother."

"I wish we didn't have to."

"It's better if you call her than if we do. What do you really think happened to her?" the policeman asked.

"No idea," Victor said.

"I'm thinking she found out that she was pregnant. She thought about what to do next." Emma was thinking out loud. "We both work at the hospital; she didn't want to go there. She was afraid we'd find out. She went elsewhere."

"How? Does she have a car?"

"No."

"How then?"

"A friend's car. A train. Greyhound. Plane."

"Where would she go?"

"Planned Parenthood. Closest ED."

"Why?"

"To confirm the pregnancy. To get rid of it."

"Where else?"

"Her grandmother? A friend? A trip?"

"A trip where?"

"Anywhere. She loves traveling. But what if she didn't choose to leave? What if something happened to her? What if she was kidnapped or even worse? What if the father decided to get rid of her?"

"Do you have any reason to suspect that?"

Victor shrugged. Emma knew better.

Life's always there to screw you.

27

LIFE'S always there to screw you.

"Dr. Steele to Room 2."

Emma sighed and returned to here and now. *Taylor will have to wait.*

Sheila wasn't looking good. Her skin was ashen; her oxygen sats were dropping.

She's tiring out. I have to do something. Like now. Twelve more patients waiting, two of whom I haven't seen. I hope they're breathing. They'll call me if they die. If they notice.

She paged the ICU and the renal attending for Sheila, then went looking for Sal. She walked into Judy, who was charge nurse today.

"Can you call Dr. Crump and tell him that his wife is in the ED? She'd like to see him."

Judy looked put out.

She thinks that I should call him myself. She's right. I should; I just can't. Not right now.

She sighed and walked away. Faith had called the Poison Control Center and they had recommended activated charcoal, even though the ingestion was hours old.

It's late for that, but aspirin overdoses are dangerous. Tablets stick together in clumps, and they get stuck in the stomach for hours. The activated charcoal helps eliminate them. It may not help her, but it can't hurt.

"How can I help?" Sal asked.

"We need a bicarb drip for Room 2."

"Renal failure?"

"Aspirin overdose."

"I haven't seen one of those in ages. Acute or chronic?"

Most aspirin overdoses were chronic. Elderly folks who forgot they took their pills, so they took them again. And again. They got weak and dizzy, like every other patient, every single shift. Easy to miss. Not this one.

"Acute, intentional."

"Wow. Do we know how much and when?"

"Last night. She took a handful, whatever that means."

"Did she take anything else?"

"Not that we know of."

"OK, I'll get the bicarb. That will help alkalinize her urine and enhance elimination. By the way, Dr. Steele, did you hear yesterday's case?"

That's never good news.

"Not yet. What was it?"

"Another Narcan-resistant overdose. They gave him four doses before he responded."

"Did he make it?"

"He made it to the ICU."

"Have you heard any more from your Poison Control Center friend?

"I'm meeting her tonight. You want to come?"

"Not tonight. Thanks, Sal. Please keep me posted. And let's get that drip going, shall we?"

"It's on its way."

She started Sheila on bipap, a plastic mask covering her mouth and nose, pushing air into her lungs to give her breathing muscles some rest. *She's looking better.*

Still no Kurt.

"No answer. I left a message. Should I try Kayla?" Judy asked.

So that's public knowledge. Is that why Sheila overdosed?

The speakers saved her again.

"Dr. Steele to Room 3."

The man in Room 3 had "the look." Pale, ashen, clutching his chest with calloused hands, wide eyes staring into death. *The poster child for a heart attack.*

"How long have you had this pain?"

The man groaned.

Confused?

Sweat poured out of him. They tried to wipe him off, but the EKG leads still wouldn't stick. The CNA tried holding them down with tape. No good. Brenda got IV access. They gave him aspirin and nitroglycerin.

That helped with the pain. He started talking.

The pain started last night as he was cutting wood—bad news. It's been waxing and waning through the night. He's short of breath—more bad news. He's fifty and a smoker; his father had his first heart attack at thirty-eight. More and more bad news.

The EKG was nondiagnostic. Not normal, but not a STEMI either.

"Let's send a cardiac panel. Please get another EKG in ten minutes."

The second EKG hadn't changed much. She signed it, timed it, and asked for another in ten minutes.

"Why? What's wrong with this one?" Aisha, the CNA, frowned.

"There's nothing wrong with it, but I need to see if anything changes. We need to know if he gets worse."

It did.

She paged cardiology. It was Victor.

"I have something for you," she said.

"So do I. We found Taylor."

Emma's breath caught in her chest.

Alive or dead?

Her throat was too tight to speak.

"She's safe."

28

"WHERE IS SHE?"

"With Mother, in Atlanta."

"Margret said she wasn't there."

"She lied. Amber made her promise, and she didn't want to break her trust."

"How is she?"

"Pregnant. Otherwise fine."

"How pregnant?"

"Don't know. Early, Mother says."

"How did you find out?"

"Mother talked her into calling me. She wants to get an abortion."

"An abortion?!" Emma was not religious, not in the least, but she was a doctor. She was committed to saving lives. She'd thought about Taylor's pregnancy, but mainly she'd worried about her safety. She had nightmares about her lying dead in a ditch.

"An abortion," Victor said.

That was not an option as far as Victor was concerned; he was a practicing Catholic. For him, there was no bigger sin. Nine years ago, when he left Emma to marry Amber, it had been because of Amber's unplanned pregnancy.

Unplanned, my ass, Amber knew damn well what she was doing when she forgot to take that pill.

"Who's the father?"

"She wouldn't tell me." Victor choked. "She can't have an abortion, Emma, she'll never forgive herself."

Emma wasn't so sure.

"She's just seventeen. What will happen to her future? To her college?"

"She'll manage somehow. Many girls do! You and I will help."

"Oh no, not me!" Emma shuddered. "One child was more than enough for me; I can't even think about having another baby in the house."

"She's your daughter! She needs your help, Emma! You can't abandon her!"

"I know. I can't abandon her, but I can tell you right now that I can't bring up her child. Not me. Maybe Amber?"

"Amber??!"

"Or you?"

The silence at the other end was long and ominous.

"We'll cross that bridge when we get to it," he finally said. "We need to get her home."

"Why? She's better off with your mother."

Margret, Victor's mother, was a real southern lady. Perfectly groomed and infallibly polite, she was a nice person and a great cook. She lived alone in a large house in the suburbs of Atlanta. Emma thought she looked like the aging version of Melanie Wilkes from *Gone with the Wind*—beautiful, dignified, kind.

"She likes your mother. Margret will be kind to her. It

will allow her to think things through better than if she were here."

"Are you trying to pawn her off?"

"I didn't send her there. She chose to go. She may be happier there."

"We need to talk to her at least!"

"That we do. Tomorrow I only have one meeting. I can cancel it. Should we fly there?"

"OK. I'll get tickets."

"I'll get something for your mother."

Taylor couldn't find a better place to be. Maybe some of Margret's class and kindness will rub off on her.

Fat chance!

29

EMMA WRAPPED her extra shirt around Margret's present—a blown glass vase. It looked like a Greek museum artifact, with its stunted shape and irregular haziness.

She should get something for Taylor, too, she thought, but she couldn't come up with anything. Moreover, she had few good feelings about Taylor right now. Now that she was safe, she could go back to remembering what a pain in the ass she was.

She'd been a difficult baby, then grew into a stubborn toddler in a perpetual temper tantrum. She was a pain. Other mothers seemed to get along with their children. They even seemed to like them. Emma didn't like Taylor.

She loved her, of course—not like she had a choice, she had to love her, motherly love and all that crap—but she preferred dogs. Even cats. They may be ungrateful, but at least they weren't evil.

She added her *Neurological Emergencies* book to her pack for a little light reading and poured herself a glass of Medoc, a Chateau Greysac 2012, not too expensive but with the distinctive lingering tannins all Bordeaux share. She'd earned it.

The day had been rough. Still, she hadn't killed anyone. That she knew of. Victor had taken the chest pain to the cath lab. He needed stents, and he needed them now.

"Good catch," he said.

He wasn't kidding. That one she'd earned her money on.

Sheila had been another matter.

Kurt arrived hours later. He wasn't happy. He was mad at Emma and the nurses. He was mad at Sheila. Most of all he was mad at himself.

"What did you do for her?" he barked.

Sheila had given her permission to tell him.

"Charcoal..."

"Charcoal won't help. It's too late!"

"The Poison Control Center recommended it."

"What else?"

"I put her on bipap. She was having trouble breathing. I gave her fluids. I started a bicarb drip. I called the intensivist and renal."

"Are they coming?"

"They've been here already. She doesn't need dialysis, not yet."

"Who's admitting her?"

"The ICU."

He clenched his teeth so tight that his jaw muscles twitched. He left without another word and went to sit with Sheila. He accompanied her to the ICU.

An hour later Emma found him sitting in her chair.

I hope he isn't going to blow up again, right here, in the middle of the ED.

He looked awful. His face flushed, his hair a mess, he looked like he'd been crying.

"How is she?" Emma asked.

"She seems OK."

"Dialysis?"

"Not yet."

"Good."

They won't have to shove that damn dialysis hose into her. That'll save her from bleeding like stink after that boatload of aspirin killed all her platelets.

Kurt stood in front of her, checking out his hands. They were shaking. He looked her in the eye. His bloodshot eyes were hurting. His attitude was gone.

"Thank you, Emma. Thank you for everything you did for Sheila. I couldn't have done better."

"It was my pleasure. I'm happy that she's doing well."

"Thanks to you." He turned around and left.

Is that an olive branch? Truce, maybe?

Wouldn't that be good!

Back to the present, she got back to her packing. Motrin, Tylenol, instant coffee, chocolate. Books.

Taylor's room was still a mess. She couldn't bring herself to clean up. Who cared? She'd closed the door and pretended that it didn't exist. Unmade bed. Books. DVDs. Mismatched shoes all over the floor. *Harry Potter and the Chamber of Secrets*, Taylor's favorite book, sat on the bedcover. Emma took it.

She'll love it.

30

THE TAXI STOPPED at Margret's door. Emma inhaled the smell of moist earth and spring. Margret's well-loved garden was waking up. The green tips of daffodils broke through the dirt. Birds called love messages. Branches shimmered green. Emma loved spring. A time for hope and joy. The wonder of new beginnings. Then she remembered Taylor's pregnancy and she shuddered.

Margret smelled like cookies and oolong tea. Her hug felt like home. She was perfect from head to toe, as usual, her well-tamed white hair framing her narrow face, her sea-green dress hugging her delicate frame, her lipstick a magnolia shade of pink.

"How was the flight?" she asked, pouring the tea they had both declined in thin porcelain cups.

"OK. How are you, Mother?" Victor asked.

He loved her dearly, but he never called her Mom. Their relationship was warm but formal. Emma wondered sometimes if she was closer to Margret than Victor was.

"I'm well. It's been a pleasure to have Taylor here."

Really?

"I'm glad to hear. How is she?"

"Better. She was a little stressed out when she arrived. She was tired, too. She hitchhiked most of the way."

"She what?" Victor choked on his tea.

Margret gave him a Mona Lisa smile.

"Hitchhiked. Your daughter has an adventurous spirit. I wonder who she takes after."

"Not me," Victor said.

"Why did she hitchhike instead of flying or taking a train?" Emma asked.

"To make it harder for you to find her. She wasn't ready to talk to you."

Margret poured another cup of tea.

"I had a hard time persuading her to call you," she told Victor. She turned to Emma. "She refused to call you. Please be kind to her, both of you. She needs some love."

What she needs is a good spanking. She's needed that for a long time.

"Of course," said Victor. "Can we see her?"

Margret called upstairs. "Taylor, your parents would like to speak to you."

She sat back drinking her tea with small ladylike sips. Her job was done.

Taylor came down two cups later.

Her long dark hair falling over her face and the over-sized checkered shirt made her look childish and fragile. So did her bare feet. She sat next to Margret, crossing her legs under her without acknowledging her parents.

Pain in the ass.

Victor got up and hugged her. After a moment she hugged him back.

Emma watched.

"How are you, sweetheart?" Victor asked.

"I'm OK," she said, playing with a rip in her jeans.

Victor looked at her, at his mother, at Emma.

"We love you, you know. We're here to help."

The silence hurt.

Emma couldn't take it anymore.

"How pregnant are you?"

"Emma!" Victor was shocked.

Taylor wasn't.

"I don't know," she said. "Two months, maybe more."

"Did you see a doctor?"

"No."

"We made an appointment for this afternoon," Margret intervened. "I thought you'd like to be with her."

Victor shrank.

"Of course," Emma lied. She couldn't pawn that off on Margret. "If Taylor wants us."

Taylor shrugged.

"Who's the father?" Emma asked.

Taylor looked her in the eye. Margret sipped on her tea.

Nobody spoke.

"I want an abortion."

"Taylor, you don't know what you're talking about. You can't have an abortion!" Victor said.

"Why not?"

"That's a baby growing inside you! You can't kill him!"

"Why not? It's not a baby; it's just an embryo. It's not alive. It's just a few hundred cells."

"It's about to become a baby, like you were! You can't kill it!"

"Yes, I can. I wish you'd killed me when I was like this!" she blurted, looking at Emma.

Emma's heart shrank. She had wished it too, many

times. Now, looking at her beautiful, difficult, and unhappy daughter, she knew that her thoughts were a sin.

"Taylor, think about Opal and Iris! This baby's going to be just like them! You can't kill him," Victor said.

That gave Taylor a moment of pause. She loved Iris and Opal; she'd been there when Amber was pregnant with them, and she'd held them when they were just a day old, no larger than a cat, innocent, vulnerable, and with a future of endless possibilities.

"This is not a baby; it's an embryo. It's not yet alive. And it won't be if I can help it. I don't need a baby. I can't even take care of myself," she said bitterly, with an insight Emma didn't know she had.

"You could give it up for adoption," Margret said. "Many families are desperately looking for a baby to love and care for."

They all stared at her. They hadn't thought of that.

"No." Taylor shook her head. "I don't wanna be pregnant and waddle around, like Amber did. I don't want to be sick all the time. I don't want people gossiping behind my back."

"You could stay here with me. Your friends would never know unless you chose to tell them."

So kind of Margret to offer.

Taylor had never been easy to live with. Her pregnancy wasn't going to make it any easier.

"No. I want an abortion."

"How about the father?" Emma asked. "Does he know? Does he agree? After all, it's his baby too."

Taylor gave her a dark look.

Victor brightened. "Yes, it's his baby too. How do you think I would have felt if Amber had gone to get an abortion without telling me?"

"First, if she didn't tell you, you wouldn't have known.

You wouldn't have felt anything. Second, you'd still be home with me and Mom instead of abandoning us like you did. I see it as a plus."

Wow!

Victor was silenced. Margret fidgeted with her cup.

Vintage Taylor. After years of blaming me for Victor's desertion, she admits that he abandoned us. All this time, she knew. She blamed me anyhow.

"I want an abortion. Whether you help me or not, I'll get it." She turned to Emma. "You know what it's like to have a child that you don't want and have your whole life ruined because of it. You need to help me."

Margret intervened. "Taylor, you are mistaken. Your mother loves you, whether you understand it or not. You haven't ruined her life."

"Not yet. One way or another, I'll get an abortion; I don't care if I bleed to death. I'll still get it. You won't look so good if your daughter dies because of poor medical care, Dr. Steele, will you?" she asked, her eyes dark with hate.

"Your reputation will be over, your career may be over, and you won't feel too good about yourself, either."

Suddenly, the harpy melted and she started crying, her childish body shaking with sobs.

"You must help me, Mother."

Emma's heart broke.

31

THEY DIDN'T TALK MUCH on the way back. There wasn't much left to say. Taylor was about six weeks pregnant. That gave her a little time to get an abortion. She needed parental consent. Victor wasn't going to give it. He thought this was all a childish folly. Taylor would fall in love with her baby as soon as she saw it.

Emma knew better. It was on her now.

She could help Taylor get an abortion. That may open the door for a lifetime of regrets and guilt. She could refuse, and risk Taylor getting a backdoor abortion.

She'd risk an infection, sterility, even death. Even if it goes well, she's going to think that I wasn't there for her when she needed me most. There's no good way out.

Victor drove her to her car.

"You can't do that, Emma. She'll never recover from it. One day she'll accuse you of killing her baby!"

"Of course she will! It's all my fault, bringing her to life, you deserting her nine years ago, Mike's death. No matter what goes wrong in Taylor's world, it's always my fault."

"But Emma, this is a baby! This is you, and me, and Taylor, all together! You can't help kill it!"

"I don't plan to. I don't do abortions. She's old enough to make her own decisions and live with the consequences. Her pregnancy is not my problem. She is. I'm trying to keep her alive."

Victor wasn't happy. He stopped next to Emma's car, alone in the hospital parking lot. It was past midnight.

"I hope you'll reconsider. I think you're making a mistake."

"I'm sorry. I'll think about it. Thanks for the ride." She opened the door and pushed the button on her key.

Her Hyundai lit up like a Christmas tree.

She stepped toward the door.

A shadow moved.

She opened the door and dashed in. She slammed it closed and locked it.

It was cold.

Victor waited.

She wondered if he'd noticed the shadow.

It was limping.

It looked familiar.

She drove home and bolted the door.

SPIDER

I'm cold.
The car sat there the whole day.
Is she ever going home?
I'm frozen. I have to go.
A car.
I move into the shade and wait.
She comes out.
I grab the knife.
She looks at me.
The other car's still there.
Waiting.
I fade into the darkness.
I'll be back.

32

EMMA SPENT the night tossing and turning and woke up haggard. She downed two double espressos to unclump enough to figure out her day.

She had a staff meeting, then a shift. A long day coming. No sleep in sight. Coffee would have to do.

She brushed her teeth twice to get rid of last night's stale wine taste. She put on scrubs. Better than looking for something that fit.

She'd gained weight. The junk food in the break room, the lack of sleep and exercise, the wine, her most important food group lately—*it counts as five daily servings of fruit*—none of that helped. The pounds had been piling on.

The worn-out woman in the mirror looked nothing like she used to. She didn't like her. She didn't love her, either.

She didn't think much about herself. Not unless she did something really special, like saving a life or making a challenging diagnosis. *You're only as good as the last thing you've done. I haven't done much lately. Struggling to barely stay afloat.*

She topped the scrubs with a fresh white coat to cover the bulges. She put on her "Chocolate Dream" red lipstick for a little boost of confidence. She added a touch of red to her cheeks, trying to look less dead. She grabbed her bag with the never-without gadgets and headed out.

The car was cold. She pulled on her mittens and gathered her rust-colored parka around her. She turned on the sound system to a lecture on pediatric trauma and drove off.

Something felt wrong.

The cold? The hunger?

The lack of sleep.

Maybe.

Just jittery from too much coffee.

The staff meeting with her former friends?

No.

Something was wrong.

The window.

She'd been driving the wet, salty roads for weeks now. The car was covered in dirt. All of it. The wipers had cleared just enough windshield to let her drive.

The driver's window had a clear patch.

Right there, to her left.

Somebody had cleaned the window just enough to look inside.

She shrugged.

There's nothing worth stealing, not even the car.

Still...

Her gut told her that something was wrong.

Her gut never lied.

Last night's shadow...

She shivered.

33

SHE WAS LATE. The staff meeting was about to start. Mike, the ED nursing director, gave her a meaningful look. She took an empty chair near Brenda, who ignored her.

"Thank you all for coming," Mike opened. "I have good news. George is better."

Cheers erupted. George was well loved. He'd been a mentor to many, and a friend to all.

"He has become more responsive. He's now alert when they lighten his sedation. They hope to extubate him in a day or two. That's the best news we've had since his accident."

Accident?! That's a misnomer. Everybody knows it was attempted murder; police have been here daily looking into everything, asking questions, collecting fingerprints and whatever else they collect.

"Jennie is collecting money for his family. Whoever wants to donate, please see her. Every little bit helps, even if it's just gas money."

Noise increased as people reached for their money. Mike raised his voice.

"Our second issue today is Narcan. We've been using more Narcan in the first two months of this year than throughout half of last year. We're running out. We tried to contact new vendors and see if the Health Department can help us, but for now we have to conserve it. Please don't use it unless you have to."

The room exploded into indignant vociferations.

"You've got to be kidding!" Suzy said. "How would we know if we need it unless we see if it works or not?"

"Yeah, really! Are you serious? You want to ration the Narcan now?" Carlos, who never spoke, now did. He'd come from New Hampshire, the epicenter of the opioid epidemic. They practically lived on Narcan.

"This is madness," Kurt said. "Narcan's not only a treatment, it's a diagnostic tool. Narcan is part of the ACLS protocol. We won't know if we really need it until we see if it works or not."

"We need to get more," Brenda said. She turned to Sal, who was trying to blend into the background. As the ED pharmacist, he was the go-to person for Narcan.

"Cool down, everybody," Mike said. "I didn't say you shouldn't use it. I just said use it more judiciously. There've been a number of cases—six, to be precise—of patients receiving more than two doses of Narcan. That's not part of the ACLS protocol nor is it standard of care."

"Really? More than two doses?" Kurt asked.

He'd aged. Emma hadn't seen him since the day Sheila overdosed. She had wondered how she was doing. She wanted to check, but she was afraid to antagonize Kurt again.

He looks just as miserable as I feel.

"Yes, three doses in three cases, four in two more, and in

one case the patient received six doses of Narcan. That's not in any guidelines."

"That's true," Kurt agreed. "Who gave that and why?"

"I did," said Emma. "The patient was a healthy young man with a presentation typical for an overdose, so I gave him some more. He didn't respond, so I gave him even more."

"Six doses?"

"Yes."

"Did it work?"

"Yes. The patient had return of spontaneous circulation and went to the ICU."

"That's nice, but then what? Restarting the heart is no good if the brain doesn't make it. Putting brain-dead patients in the ICU is only draining our meager resources. The only thing that really matters is a good neurologic outcome. Did he make it to discharge?"

I wish I knew. With Taylor and everything else, I forgot to check on the kid. He was down for so long that even if he's alive he's probably neurologically devastated.

"He was discharged yesterday," Sal said. "He walked out. He was completely normal."

"Really!" Kurt said. "How much Narcan did you say you gave him?

"Six doses, I think."

"Why?"

"It just looked like it should work. Young, healthy, looked like an OD." Emma hesitated, then continued, "I thought it may be fentanyl. I think we have somebody selling fentanyl in our community."

A heavy silence fell. Fentanyl was potent and dangerous. Fentanyl on the street was bad news.

"Was he positive for fentanyl?" Kurt asked.

"Yes."

"Why that much Narcan, though?" Brenda asked.

Sal answered: "Because of its affinity to the opioid receptors. It binds much tighter. You need to overflow it with Narcan to dislodge it and reverse its effects. The only good news is that it wears off fast, so you usually don't need to repeat the dose."

"You mean after the first six?" Brenda asked, and they all laughed.

Life in the ED is rough. People suffer; people die. Bad news and tragedies are a dime a dozen; the only way to make it through is to grow a thick skin and have a sick sense of humor. We laugh at things that nobody else finds funny; otherwise, we'd cry. It's like being at war. There are no guns, but it's just like M*A*S*H: suffering, death, and weirdos.

"This is bad news," Kurt said. "Bad for our community and bad for us."

"Is it confirmed?" Mike asked.

"Not yet," Sal said, "I'm waiting for an answer from the Poison Control Center. We sent them some samples from our cases."

"Well then," Mike said, "we'll have to wait for an answer first."

"Better get some more Narcan in the meantime," Kurt said. "You've been forewarned. If somebody dies for lack of Narcan, it will fall on you."

He still remembers our old fight. They had disagreed about triaging ambulances. A patient died. Kurt got blamed. He blamed Emma. That led to years of bad blood between them. *Is the armistice over?*

Kurt made a strong enemy. That, she could do without. She had nothing but enemies in the ED lately; even old friends like Alex, Brenda, and Judy had been avoiding her.

She headed to the door. Kurt's clear metallic voice cut through the noise.

"Dr. Steele."

I hope he's not going to embarrass both of us.

"Thank you for telling us. I'll be happy to work with you to make our ED even better."

Emma blushed. Her eyes welled with tears. She had expected anything but that. This was not an armistice, it was a full capitulation. Sal smiled. Her old friend Brenda, who had ignored her throughout the meeting, hugged her.

"I'm so proud of you!"

The cease-fire was on.

For now.

SPIDER

She's coming.
She's in the doorway, soaking the light.
I'm outside, in the dark.
She can't see me. I'm the shadow of a shadow.
She steps out.
Fish-knife in hand, I'm ready.
She looks at me.
She can't see me.
I hold my breath.
She sniffs the air.
What's she smelling? The snow?
She looks at me. She knows.
She steps back.
I shiver.
She knows I'm here.
She can't.
I wait.
She's back.
She just forgot something.
I'm ready.

She steps out.

I move closer.

Behind her, the security guards. Flashlights break the darkness, chasing me. I drop to the ground. I roll. Behind one car, then another, then another.

Basic training. Thanks, Vietnam.

She leads them to where I was.

I'm not there anymore.

She sniffs the air and looks straight at me.

She can't see me. I'm darker than dark.

She knows I'm here.

How?

I run.

I'm not going after her again.

She's a witch.

34

KAYLA PUT AWAY THE MASCARA. She took a last look in the mirror, then pulled on her furry Cossack hat. It made her look like a ginger cat. She laughed and looked out the window.

Eden was ready, playing in the snow. With his red hat and flushed cheeks, he looked happy and healthy. She was happy that Dick had asked her to bring him along. They never had enough time together, but today was Sunday, she had the day off, and they were going ice fishing.

They'd never done it before. They had seen the fishermen sitting on their upturned buckets for hours. They held their poles and looked mesmerized at a hole in the ice, waiting for the fish to bite. She'd always wondered what was so exciting about it. It couldn't be the fish; they were smaller than Eden's hand.

So what? The weather was spectacular; the frozen lake shone like scattered diamonds in the morning. Being outdoors made her feel alive!

She started the car and noticed the pile of discarded

tissues on the floor. They were left over from Friday, when Kurt had broken up with her.

He'd been avoiding her. He barely ever spoke to her, even at work. She'd tried to be understanding. She knew that his wife was sick. She respected the fact that he chose to spend time with her, but she missed him.

Eventually, she'd asked him out. He had agreed with the enthusiasm one would only reserve for a root canal.

They met for drinks at the inn across the lake, where nobody knew them.

She'd ordered coffee. She was half done with it by the time he arrived. He looked handsome and determined, just like he had on their first date, two years ago. Then, his smile lit the room. Now, his face was solemn and dark. Just like that, Kayla knew it was over.

He smiled but didn't kiss her. He sat and drank down his water to soften his throat. He looked inside his glass, staring at the half-melted ice cubes as if he were reading someone's fortune.

Mine.

He looked at her, his eyes windows into pain.

"It's over, Kayla."

"Why?"

"I can no longer do this to my wife. I love you very much; you've been the light of my life over these last two years. I just can't do this anymore. It's destroying her. That's destroying me."

"It took you a while to figure that out."

"I'm sorry to hurt your feelings."

"How about behaving like a man? How about talking to me rather than avoiding me, pretending that I don't exist?" People at the next table turned to stare, and Kurt shrunk in his seat.

Like all my men, he's a coward. He'd wiggle a wand and make me disappear in a puff of smoke if he could.

"I'm really sorry. I wish I had acted differently. I was infatuated with you—I still am. For whatever it's worth, I love you. You are fresh and beautiful and full of life. I love you to the point that I neglected, I almost destroyed, my wife of twenty years. She was so desperate that she tried to kill herself. She almost died." He choked.

"I've decided to make it up to her. I'll try to be a decent husband, like I haven't been for years. I don't know if our marriage can be fixed, but I'll do my best."

"How about me? Aren't you worried about me?"

"Oh, Kayla, if you only knew how much I worry about you! I'm sick with jealousy, but there's nothing I can do. I know you'll find somebody else. I hope it will be somebody who deserves you and cares for you. I hope he'll make you happy."

He stopped for a moment, making up his mind what to say next. The words came out by themselves. He could no longer hold them in.

"Please don't date Umber."

Kayla's jaw dropped. The audacity of telling her what to do and who to date after all this! Her blood boiled.

"Really? Why not? He's rich, he's handsome, he's single. What more can a girl hope for?"

"He's not for you, Kayla. You're bright and kind and innocent. He's a snake-oil salesman, a shrewd two-faced womanizer. He'll chew you up and spit you out. You deserve better."

"Unlike you, you mean? I don't think I need dating advice from you, thank you very much."

"Please listen, Kayla. Don't date Umber. There is something wrong with that man; I know it in my bones. It will be bad for you."

"Thank you for all your time and the lovely advice," Kayla said, gathering her bag and leaving a ten-dollar bill on the table—she didn't want to owe him anything, not even a coffee.

She didn't cry until the car. She cried her heart out then, a box of tissues worth.

Now, two days later, head held up proudly, she was going on a date. With Dick Umber.

She wouldn't have if it weren't for Kurt.

I hope he finds out and suffers!

SPIDER

I told him.
"Yep. She's a witch," he said.
"Sorry."
"No worries. You did well. Check under the picnic table behind the
ambulance bay."
I find it.
Welcome, heaven!

35

DICK WAS WAITING. Kayla introduced him to Eden. Always the gentleman, Eden offered a gloved hand. Dick shook it, and they started talking shop, discussing the thickness of the ice, how cold the water was, and whether perch preferred worms to grubs.

They drilled holes with the auger. They marveled at the one-foot-thick, translucent ice. It had pretty air bubbles caught inside. They hooked the bait and dropped the line. They waited.

Eden was too excited to sit. "How did you learn to ice fish?"

"My friend Joe taught me. He has a camp on Bow Lake. He took me ice fishing."

"Where's that?"

"In New Hampshire."

"Did you catch a fish?"

"I caught a small-mouth bass and a perch."

"Two?!"

Kayla listened in, enjoying the sun. Eden needed a male role model, and ice fishing was just one of the manly things she couldn't teach him. She was grateful that Dick did.

She took off her hat and let her hair fall over her shoulders. Dick smiled and touched it, his fingers caressing a silky curl, picking it up...

"A fish! A fish!" Eden screamed, holding on with both hands to his quivering pole.

Five minutes later they had recovered the fish, a scrawny silver wiggler, smaller than Eden's hand, but it was his first fish, and he was in awe. They let it swim in the water bucket. Eden watched him, trying to pet him. After he got bored, he wandered off counting holes in the ice, checking with a stick to see whether they had frozen through.

"You are beautiful, Kayla."

That's what Kurt said.

"How long are you here for?"

"I have four more shifts. I'm leaving on Friday."

"Where to?"

"Colorado, for some skiing. Want to come?"

"I can't. I have Eden."

"Bring him too."

"I have work, and he has school."

"When is he on vacation?"

"Beginning of March, I think."

"That's close enough. March skiing is the best."

That's a little fast.

"When are you coming back?"

"March, I think, then I'm going to Mexico to check on the boat. Have you ever been to Mexico?"

"Never," she said, wishing she was young and free to see the world, taste new foods, and have fun rather than go to work, take classes, and do laundry.

"Mexico is... "

The scream came from the left, where the wind was coming from. Eden was lying on the ice, screaming.

Kayla sprinted. Dick got there first. Eden was lying on his back on a patch of snow, his left leg gone.

Kayla bit her lip and watched Dick kneeling next to Eden. "It's all right, buddy, you're OK. What happened?"

"I can't get up!"

Eden was laying on his back. His right leg was bent. His left leg looked like it ended at the knee. Dick pushed the snow away with his gloved hands to uncover the crevasse. It went all the way through to the water. It wasn't much more than a couple inches wide, but it had been wide enough to let Eden's foot fall through and get stuck. He was trapped.

"Are you hurt?" Dick asked.

"Yes... no... I don't know! I can't get up."

"We'll fix that," Dick said. He laid on his stomach, sliding his hand along Eden's left leg as far as he could, palpating as he went.

"Good job, buddy. It all looks good; the knee seems OK, the bone is in one piece, and the foot..." He pulled his arm out.

"The foot looks OK, but I can't reach it. It won't come back out the way it went in. Kayla, go get me the ice auger and call 911."

"What's 911?" Eden asked.

"The emergency number we call when people get hurt. It brings help. You'll see."

He took the auger and started drilling carefully around the leg to enlarge the crevasse.

"We'll get you out of here in no time, and you'll have the best story to tell your friends. Want to know where the hole came from?"

Eden nodded.

"Ice expands and contracts when the temperature changes. When it gets too big, it breaks. Then, as it contracts again, it leaves a hole.

"I'm cold," Eden sobbed.

"Sure you are. I'm cold, too." The icy water dripping from his drenched sleeve was already freezing. "We'll be home soon, and we'll have some hot chocolate. You like hot chocolate?"

"I like ice cream better."

"Me too, but I think hot chocolate works better today."

He looked at the holes he'd drilled around Eden's leg. He put the auger aside and got his arm back in, now reaching deep enough to untie Eden's boot.

Eden was out when the ambulance arrived. His foot was blue with cold, but he was smiling, holding on to his new best friend. Kayla remembered Kurt's words: "He'll hurt you!"

She fell asleep dreaming of Mexico.

SPIDER

Snow.
Falling softly inside.
Through my eyes.
Through my mouth.
Through my soul.
I'm white inside.
It's been the highest high.
Can't move.
Can't breathe.
Can't cry.
Just the white sky.
Lying ice-colored eye.
Get him, witch.
I count on you.
I love you, Jessy.
I'm the snow.
I fly.

36

EMMA WAS WRAPPING up to go home when they called the code. Her shift was over, but she went to help.

"Found in the snow. No known downtime. No pulse."

"Any history?" Ann asked, as they unloaded.

"None. We couldn't get an IV; he's got track marks everywhere. We got an IO in the left tibia. We gave three doses of epi. No response."

"How long ago was he found?"

"Thirty minutes. No bystander CPR. We got him eighteen minutes ago."

"Cardiac activity?"

"PEA, pulseless electric activity, only."

"Get a rectal temp," Sue ordered.

The angry monitors rang like chime-bells in a hurricane with the 120 beats/second of the CPR. The body lay quietly. His face was blue and gaunt, his eyes open, his huge pupils unreactive.

He's dead. But it's not my call. He's Ann's patient. She'll call it when she's ready.

Emma grabbed her trauma shears and cut through his

right sleeve to expose the arm. His coat, once pink, was filled with down. Stirred by the air movement, white feathers swirled softly, falling slowly and quietly like fresh snow.

She cut through the wet navy sweater underneath to the skin. His bony hand was blue with cold, but the blue spider tattoo stretching its legs over the dirty fingers was hard to miss.

The Spider.

37

EMMA SIGNED out to Alex one hour late.

"How's Taylor?"

"She's OK; she's spending some time with her grandmother."

"Teenagers are tough. You look like you could use some sleep," he said, looking in her eyes as if he knew.

He can't, can he? She remembered that his daughter Karen was Amber's best friend.

"Let me know if I can help."

"I will, thank you." She turned to leave and walked straight into Detective Zagarian.

He looked overdressed in his well-cut gray suit, light gray shirt, and burgundy tie with gold flecks. His inscrutable eyes were also gray.

The gray man. Unobtrusive. Dangerous.

"I've been waiting for you. They said you'd be done at four."

It was ten past five. She'd had to stay over to clean up. She'd finally admitted the demented patient whose family refused to take him home. She had found a pediatrician for the wheezing toddler whose mother had no insurance. She had discharged the woman with chronic pain she just couldn't sign out.

"I had to tie up some loose ends. What can I do for you?"

"Do you have time to go for a coffee or a drink?"

"Why?"

It had been another rough shift after a rough night after a rough day. She was looking forward to some peace and quiet. And wine.

"To chat."

He smiled; his eyes smiled, too, and told her she was pretty. They lied. She hadn't been pretty in the morning when she'd put on makeup and lipstick; that had been many patients ago. *I hate to think about how I must smell.*

"Is this personal or professional?"

"A little bit of both."

She looked at her scrubs. *That's no cocktail attire. If I don't talk to him now, he'll be back. May as well get this out of the way.*

Half an hour later they sat at a table for two at Luigi's, looking over the frozen lake. Emma held her steaming coffee with both hands to warm her fingers. It was cold in the ED, so cold that her fingers hurt and she could barely type. She was frozen to the core.

"What can I do for you?"

She kept her jacket on to hide her scrubs. She felt out of place amongst the loud, well-dressed crowd. *They had too much wine. I wish I'd said no and gone home. I'd be drinking wine too.*

"I wondered if you remembered anything. Any ideas about who wanted to kill the nurse? Or about the source of that money?"

"No, I didn't." Between Taylor and her patients, she'd had plenty to worry about.

"Any ideas of where that propofol could have come from?"

Emma shook her head no.

"It was part of a batch that was shipped to five hospitals in New Hampshire, six months ago. Also a couple of places in California. We're trying to pin down exactly where this particular bottle went. Does that ring a bell?"

"Nope."

"Well, let that sink in. Maybe something will come to you." He took a sip of coffee and grimaced. "This'll put you to sleep rather than wake you up."

"That's good, since it's almost bedtime."

"Oh, it's a little early for that. Are you married?"

"No. Are you?"

"Not lately. My ex-wife and I get along better now than when we were married."

"It happens."

"Yes, it's always easier when you don't have skin in the game."

"Kids?"

"Two. Twenty and twenty-two. Both in college. You?"

"One daughter, seventeen."

"Lives with you?"

"She's with her grandmother for the moment."

"That's a difficult age."

If one more person tells me that teenagers suck, I'm going to blow up.

"I couldn't help but notice."

He took the hint.

"Tell me about propofol."

"It's a wonderful drug. For procedural sedation, mostly.

They call it "Milk of Amnesia" because it's milk-white and makes patients amnestic. Once you give it, they don't remember anything else. They wake up after the procedure, asking when we're going to start. It takes about a minute to start working, and it wears off in eight minutes or so— except for kids, they burn through it like crazy. It puts the patients to sleep, so you can relocate their hips or put in a chest tube or intubate them. It's a fantastic drug, but if you give too much, they stop breathing. That's what happened to Michael Jackson. It also drops their blood pressure. That's why you need to watch them like a hawk."

"How long would the nurse have been out for?"

"His name is George."

"How long would George have been out for?"

"It depends on how much he got. Eight, ten minutes maybe? If he stopped breathing, he could be gone for good."

"Let's talk this through. Whoever did this, they had to get in an IV.

Emma nodded.

"After that, they had to push the drug. Then it takes another minute to work?"

"Yes."

"How long would it all take?"

"Depends on the veins and the skill level. Three minutes or so?"

"Could that happen if he was conscious?"

"No. He'd fight, he'd scream..."

"Yes, but who would hear? Plus, the showers are locked. They couldn't get in without the code."

"They could call security."

"Unless they thought it was just another lunatic screaming in the ED."

"We call them patients, you know."

"Another patient screaming in the ED. Do women use the same shower?"

"Of course not."

"Is the code the same?"

Emma shrugged. "Probably not, but we can find out."

"I already did; it's not. So it must have been a man."

So why ask me?

"What was George doing in the shower? Was his shift over?"

"No, but if you get sprayed with blood or other body fluids, you need to get changed. It happens."

"Fair enough. I spoke to the nurses who worked with him that day. Nobody noticed anything like that happening. If he went to take a shower or get changed, he'd have told somebody he was off the floor, wouldn't he?"

"Probably. His partner and the charge nurse. Somebody would have had to keep an eye on his patients."

"He didn't. So he went there for some other reason. He didn't expect to be gone long. My theory is that he went there to meet the guy we're looking for. They wanted privacy. To exchange money. Maybe drugs. The other person got close enough to grab him by the throat and choke him—how long does it take to become unconscious when you're choked?"

"Seconds, if they press on your carotids to shut down the blood flow to the brain."

"He then smashed George's head on the concrete corner to keep him unconscious. He put in an IV and then pushed the propofol in—a big enough dose to stop his breathing. He left the needle there to make it look like the nurse... like George had shot it himself. Now it's just an accidental overdose. Does this make sense from a medical point of view?"

"It does, except... I don't think George was blackmailing anybody. It's not like him."

"People never cease to surprise me. It's hard to tell what somebody will do if they have a good reason."

"Did you find any material evidence?"

"We found all sorts of material evidence—hairs, fibers, blood—like you would find in a shower that fifty people use every day. We don't know which is relevant to our case."

"Anything to suggest that George put up a fight?"

Zagarian took another sip of coffee and asked, "Wanna have some dinner?"

She was about to say no, when her stomach reminded her that she hadn't eaten since breakfast. *There's no food at home. I'm finally warm, sitting in my favorite restaurant, and I'm going home hungry?*

"Why not?" She loosened her jacket and her scrubs peeked through. "Sorry for my outfit."

"You'll dress up next time." He signaled the waiter.

Next time? "The Shrimp a la Luigi is great. So is the chicken."

"Shrimp then. How about some wine?"

"They have a nice crisp Marlborough sauvignon blanc by the glass."

"You're not up for a bottle?"

"Not before driving home in the snow."

They ate and drank in pleasant companionship. The flavors of bacon, garlic, and charred meat streaming from the kitchen made her mouth water. The sauvignon blanc, a yellow so pale it was almost clear, was citrusy and light, its dry crispness a palate cleanser after the creamy richness of the shrimp. They talked about work and about their love for travel and food, avoiding personal things like exes and kids.

He's attractive and funny. She relaxed and made the wine last. Suddenly he came back to business.

"Why would George blackmail somebody? What could be important enough to make him forget his principles?

"Mary and the kids. If they were in trouble, George would do anything to get them out."

"Are they in trouble?"

"Not that I know of. Just the ordinary struggles to pay the bills, but they've been like that for years."

"Could he have a lover?"

Emma shrugged. "Who knows?"

The waiter brought the bill, and Emma tried to pay her share but he declined.

"I'll expense this," he said, making it clear that it had been just business.

Oh well. Emma drove home thinking about George.

38

SHE CALLED Mary as soon as she got home.

"How are you, Mary?"

"I'm OK. You?"

"I'm good. How's George?"

"A little better every day. They're talking about extubating him. Now he's awake when they turn down the sedation. He can't talk with that tube in his throat, but he writes notes asking about the hockey games. He must be better!"

"That's George all right! Did he tell you what happened?"

"He can't remember anything."

Of course he wouldn't, with all that propofol.

"I'm glad he's doing better. Mary, are you all right?"

"As good as I can be with all this shit hitting the fan. Better now that it looks like he's gonna make it. Can't imagine what I'd do without him."

Emma wished she'd driven to Mary rather than calling her. It would have been easier to talk, but it was late, and she was tired, and she hadn't.

"Mary, is there anything going on that would worry

George? Like really, really needing money? To the point of doing something illegal?"

"George is a good man! Whoever says he stole anything is lying!"

"I know George is a good man, Mary. He's a wonderful man and I care for him very much, but... Is there some reason he could have gotten in trouble to get money?"

Long pause, then heartbreaking sobs. Emma sat quietly, waiting.

"I have lung cancer," Mary said. "They found it in November. They said I needed surgery and chemo. Maybe radiation, they weren't sure." She started crying harder, her raw grief piercing Emma's heart.

"I have no insurance. Neither does George, but he's a vet; he gets medical care at the VA. We couldn't afford it, you know. We have no way to pay for the treatment." Her voice became a little steadier. "George said, 'Don't worry, I'll get the money.' 'How?' I asked. 'Don't worry,' he said, 'I'll find it.'"

So that's that. George found a way to get money; he black-mailed somebody who tried to kill him. But who? And why? "I'm so sorry, Mary. You're a strong woman, and you'll pull through. So will George. You are both wonderful, strong people."

"Thank you, Emma. Love you too. Stop by, will you?"

"I'll be over soon." She poured herself a glass of wine to dull the pain and help herself to sleep. She was sad enough and warm enough to open a summer wine, a Kim Crawford Marlborough sauvignon blanc from New Zealand. The pale, light yellow soon faded under the frosting of the glass. Crisp and dry, with hints of passion fruit and fresh-cut grass, it brought memories of long sunny days and hope. *Gone now. Life sucks.*

She went to bed thinking about Mary and George, about Zagarian and Victor, about Taylor and her decision to abort. *What should I do?*

The thought came to her as she was falling asleep. *Whoever George was blackmailing, how come they had propofol in their pocket ? Not even ours, but from California or New Hampshire!*

New Hampshire, where they had all those fentanyl deaths! Now we have all these Narcan-resistant overdoses! There must be a connection.

Whoever was selling fentanyl in New Hampshire came here to open shop. George found out something and blackmailed them, so they decided to kill him.

This has got to be it! I'll call Zagarian in the morning!

39

SHE DIDN'T. The phone rang at 4:45, waking her up from a restless sleep populated by nightmares in which Taylor and Zagarian were fighting for a syringe loaded with fentanyl. She stumbled to answer.

"Mom, you need to come."

"Taylor?"

"Yes. You need to come."

"Come where?"

"Here, at Grandma's."

Emma looked at the clock—not quite 5:00 a.m.

"What happened?"

"Grandma."

"Yes?"

"She fell down the stairs."

"Is she hurt?"

"She doesn't answer me."

"OK, hang up and call 911. Tell them..."

"I already did. Do you think I'm stupid? They're on their way."

"OK. Did you call your father?"

"No. I called you."

That's a first.

"Are you near her? Is she breathing?"

"Yes. She also has a pulse. 58."

That's my girl. "Does she look hurt?"

"No, she looks asleep, but she can't be."

"Don't move her." Emma tried to think quickly.

"Go to her bedroom and find her medication list. The EMTs will want it. Take a picture of it with your cell phone before you give it to them so there's a copy in case it gets lost. Make sure you give them your phone number so they can call you. Better yet, write it on the medication list. Ask them what hospital they're taking her to so we can find her. Unlock the door, open it, and turn on the lights outside so they can find the house easier. Is she still breathing?"

"I don't know. I'm looking for her medication list. I found it... They're here." She hung up.

Emma shook her head to clear it. She washed her face with ice-cold water. That helped. She poured herself a mug of the coffee she'd cold-brewed the night before. She called Victor. She called the ED to let them know she was gone for the day.

She remembered about calling Zagarian on the flight to Atlanta. *I'll do it after I land.*

She forgot.

They took a taxi to the ER. Taylor was standing in the doorway. Sobbing, she rushed into Victor's arms.

He paled, his knees weak. "Is she dead?"

"No." She blew her nose. "They said she had a heart attack."

"Anything else?"

She shook her head no and sobbed, holding on to him. Emma went to the triage nurse, a tired woman whose watchful eyes saw beyond the skin.

"I'm Dr. Emma Steele."

"What can I do for you?"

"We're here for a family member, Mrs. Margret Storm."

The nurse checked the board. "Room 17," she said, letting them in.

Margret, serene and beautiful as ever, not one hair out of place, was lying in the hospital bed that they'd gotten for her instead of the backbreaking ER stretcher. She smiled and greeted them as if they were in her living room. *The only thing missing is the tea.*

"So sorry to have bothered you both. All three in fact," she said, looking at Taylor. Emma kissed Margret's cheek and made room for Victor.

"What happened, Mother?" Victor asked.

"They said I had a heart attack. I got up and I was going to make coffee; then I woke up in the ambulance."

"Are you hurt?" Emma asked, looking at her face, checking out her neck, and fighting the urge to palpate her cervical spine. *I'm not her doctor. I hope they checked her neck... and hips...*

"A few bruises here and there, not bad."

"Did they scan your head?

Margret smiled. "Sure they did, dear; they said it looks alright."

"How about the neck?"

"The neck doesn't hurt."

"Do you have any chest pain?" Victor asked. "Are you short of breath?"

"I'm OK. Both of you stop fussing; you're making me

uncomfortable." She turned to Taylor. "I wish you hadn't called them."

"I'm glad she did," Victor said. "May I have your permission to speak to your doctor?"

"Go ahead; I can't stop you. You girls, you look like you need some rest." She looked from Taylor's messy hair to Emma's wrinkled travel outfit. "I do too. Go home and catch a nap. I'll see you later."

The taxi trip was short. They sat quietly at the kitchen table, looking in their coffee cups. Taylor, who knew her way around Margret's kitchen, had made coffee. *It's awful, way too weak, but it's the first coffee Taylor's ever made for me. She's pale and thin. Morning sickness?*

"How are you?"

Taylor took a long time to respond.

"Better now that you guys are here." She took a sip of coffee and grimaced. "That's awful!"

"I've made worse," Emma said, taking another sip. "Did I ever tell you about the first time I cooked for your father?"

"No."

"He came for dinner. I found some baccalà, dried salted cod. It was easy to cook. I got basil and lemongrass and garlic and chilies. I washed it really well, and I tasted it. It tasted good."

Taylor was smiling, waiting for the punch line, and Emma, who hadn't seen her smile in a long time, wondered again at how breathtakingly beautiful she was, and how fragile.

"I baked it with the herbs and wine. It smelled heavenly. It looked good, too, with fresh herbs and lemon slices. Your father brought me roses. I served the fish on a nice white platter."

"And?"

"He tasted it and spit it back on the plate. It was so salty that we couldn't eat it. I had to throw it away. I threw it in the back yard in the compost pile."

"What did you eat, then?"

"I don't remember, but that's not the worst part. I had this one-eyed cat. Her name was Cleopatra. She loved fish.

"She found the baccalà and started eating it, salt and all. We couldn't understand why she was thirsty all the time. She'd always used to climb on the sink to get a drink, but now she was basically living in the sink. She got so heavy that I could barely pick her up. She was swollen, you see, from all the water she'd been drinking because the fish was so salty."

"Did she die?"

"Eventually, but not because of that."

They laughed and sat quietly until Taylor asked, "Are you going to help me?"

Emma didn't know.

"I wish I knew what's best for you, Taylor. I want nothing more than to help you; I'm just trying to figure out how to do that."

"I need an abortion. That's what's best for me."

"That's what you think today, and you may be right. Or not. You may come to be very sorry one day that you gave up the opportunity to have this child."

"No, I won't."

"You don't know that. You just think you do.

"I know it."

I wish I was as half as sure of anything as Taylor always is. I'm always afraid that I'm wrong. This was both a blessing and a curse—it made her a better doctor, since she always kept an open mind, but it was nerve-wracking to always wonder if you were sending somebody home to die. *Taylor has answers to everything. Some day she'll know better, and it's going to hurt.*

"Taylor, things change. People change. Look at your father and me; we never thought we'd end up divorced. Some day you may be sorry you didn't have this child. Look at the woman who helped legalize abortions in the U.S., the famous case of Roe vs. Wade; she's now fighting to overturn the law she helped create."

"I won't change my mind. I need an abortion."

"How do you know?"

Taylor stood up and poured her coffee down the drain.

"You said you wanted to know who the father was."

The silence smelled like doom.

Who could it be to matter? One of Taylor's friends, or Tom, or... Victor? She shivered and was ashamed of herself. *Things like that have happened before... But no, not Victor. That can't be.*

Her voice thin as a thread, looking down with her shoulders hunched, Taylor said: "I don't know who the father is."

What does that mean? Was there more than one guy? Did she have sex with a stranger?

"I was raped. I was at Bill's birthday party; we'd had a few drinks and then one of his friends said, 'Let's try these pills,' and we did, all eight of us, and then I don't know what happened, but the next morning I woke up in Bill's basement covered in blood down below, alone. I had never had sex before. I don't know what they did to me. I felt dirty and disgusting, I still do. And then there's this...this thing growing inside me. I can't have a child like that. I can't. I don't care if I never ever have children. I want it out."

She turned to face Emma, her tears running down her beautiful face like crystal rivers.

"Will you help me?"

Emma stood up and hugged her like she was never going to let go. Their tears ran down together.

"I'll do anything. Anything I can."

40

EMMA HANDED Mary the box of chocolates she got at the hospital gift store. George lay on the sofa, watching the game. He was tired and gaunt, but he hadn't lost the twinkle in his eye.

"Hello, stranger," he said.

"You have room to talk!" She hugged him and assessed him from head to the blanket covering his feet as if he were a patient. *He's tired. Not ill, like he's about to crash and burn, but exhausted.* She missed him.

More importantly, she needed to find out what happened. One way or another, she was going to find the drug peddler. *George knows something. I'll get him to tell me things he wouldn't tell police.*

She didn't like drug seekers. Disingenuous, demanding, and manipulative, they were nothing but trouble. *If you believe they're in pain and give them a script, you get blamed for the opioid epidemic. If you don't, you may be sending them home to die. If you don't give them their fix, they become aggressive; if you do, you're a licensed drug peddler. There's no middle ground.*

She had never thought about drug peddlers until this slew of overdoses. That had hit her hard. So many young lives destroyed! So many pointless deaths!

Taylor's story had been the last straw.

I'm going to destroy this drug peddler if it kills me. I need George to help me.

She pointed at the glass ashtray on the side table.

"When are you gonna quit?"

"I have. I just keep it here for company," he said, breaking into the irritating dry cough of quitters.

"Good for you. How are you?"

"Never better." His rogue smile uncovered his golden tooth—a souvenir from Vietnam—gleaming under his mustache. "How are you?"

"Surviving. The ED is not the same without you."

"That's good. It wasn't that great before."

"Well, it's no better now. We miss you."

"Good. I'll be back in no time."

"No, you won't," Mary said, bringing coffee. "Not if I have anything to say about it."

"But you don't, *agapi mou*," he teased her, using half of his Greek vocabulary. The rest of it was Ouzo and Retsina.

"Do you remember what happened?"

"No. I only remember the damn ICU nurses flashing lights in my eyes."

"What's the last thing you remember?"

"Walking to the showers. Checking my pocket for my cigarettes. I thought I'd catch a quick one."

"Did you ever get that cigarette?"

George shrugged.

"Why did you go to the showers?"

"To shower, I guess."

"Why?"

George looked her in the eye. "To get clean?"

"Were you dirty?"

His eyes looked through her, into his own brain, searching.

She saw the exact moment when he remembered. He looked away. He smiled. He lied.

"I don't remember. Was I?"

"You took off without telling anyone in the middle of your shift. They found you with a needle in your arm and blood in your brain. What happened?

"No idea. Bad luck, I guess." He smiled, his eyes guarded.

"That's more than bad luck. Was somebody trying to get rid of you?"

"They all do. I'm a pain in the arse."

"Having you killed is a bit extreme."

"Maybe they just tried to get me fired. Who knows?"

He's not going to tell me.

"George, this is no good. You could save lives if you spoke up."

"Who? The seekers? You wanna know what I think about them?"

"They are people, too. They have parents and husbands and families who are suffering."

"That's their problem. Their people can worry about them. I have my own to worry about." His eyes slid over to Mary.

"I'll do everything I can for Mary," Emma said.

"I know you would. But she's not yours to take care of. She's mine."

"What if next time you don't wake up? What's going to happen to Mary and the kids?"

"You have a point," he nodded. "I can take care of myself, but I'll leave you a message, just in case it turns bad."

"How?"

"I don't know, Emma. I'll figure it out. I'm sorry. We all have our crosses to bear."

41

HE's RIGHT, Emma thought on her drive home. *We all have our crosses to bear.*

Taylor had stayed in Atlanta.

"I love it here. Grandma needs me. I'll stay."

Emma knew better than to believe her.

That's bullshit. She's never sacrificed herself for anyone. She's got a plan.

Even worse, she'd asked Emma to tell Victor.

"Can you tell him? I just can't do this again."

Emma waited until the flight.

"Taylor doesn't know who the father is."

"How come?"

"She was at a party. She woke up to find out that she'd been raped."

Victor's wounded sob was the most painful sound Emma could remember. Head bent, eyes closed, he cradled his grief.

"So?" he asked.

"I promised I'd get her an abortion."

He sobbed again.

"She needs testing—HIV, hepatitis, syphilis, gonorrhea —God knows what else."

"God doesn't know. Or he doesn't care," Victor said. "No God would allow this to happen. It's all bullshit."

Emma's eyes stung.

I hoped his faith would give him solace. He lost his religion instead. No parent deserves this much pain.

In her career, she'd given bad news to so many parents. Too many to count.

The first time was a chubby toddler. He'd been tired for a week. He looked good. His labs didn't.

"Leukemia," her attending said. "That white count is too high for a random infection."

"Are we sure?"

"We're in the ER. We're never sure. Of anything. Unless they're dead. Not even then."

"How come?"

"I ran a code on the floor. After half an hour, I called it. I declared him dead. An hour later he came back to life. That made me popular. Now, they all want me to code them if they die. They think they'll live forever." His eyes bore into hers. "Emma, in emergency medicine we're never sure. We're in the business of managing risk. What are the odds that this heartburn is a heart attack? What's the chance that this fever is meningitis? Can this numbness be a stroke? We calculate probabilities. We assume risks. Can you handle this? If not, the ER is not for you."

Emma nodded.

"You have to learn to give bad news. You'll want to run away. You can't. Open yourself to the pain. Embrace it. That's the only way to help your patients."

Emma had told the parents. She sat with them. She

listened to them. She hugged them. They were heartbroken and grateful.

Afterward, she went to the bathroom to cry.

That had been long ago, before her life had hardened her.

She took Victor's hand.

I'll cry later.

42

TIME TO CALL ZAGARIAN, Emma thought. George won't talk. It's only a matter of time until the next disaster—another overdose, another rape, another attempt to silence George. Next time he may not be so lucky. She was both angry and in awe of his dedication to Mary. *I wish I had somebody to love me like that.*

Zagarian answered on the third ring. "Let's meet. Are you at home?"

"On my way."

"I'll be there in half an hour." He hung up before she could suggest another place. *No big deal. This isn't personal.* She started coffee and changed into a pink sweater. It covered her curves and gave her a nice glow. She brushed her hair. She put on lipstick. She grabbed her perfume, then felt silly and put it back.

As usual, Zagarian looked as if he'd dropped out of a magazine. She tried to hide her tired purple crocs; then, annoyed at herself, she stuck her feet out in defiance.

"Nice place," he said. He took in the deep green leather

sofa, the gas fireplace giving the room a cozy glow, and her paintings—abstract splashes of bright color, bringing life to the room. "Have you lived here long?"

"Ten years or so."

"What's new?"

"A couple of things. First a question: Did you find out where the propofol came from?"

"A critical care access hospital in New Hampshire. The batch got delivered last May, recorded as being used in July."

"By whom?"

"By a nurse in the local ED."

"Did you speak to her?"

"She's dead."

"How?"

"Overdose."

Emma let that sink in for a moment. "Propofol?"

"Fentanyl."

Fentanyl again.

"Self-inflicted?"

"Apparently. She had been using for a while. She was caught diverting drugs. She got fired. They found her dead. There was no reason to suspect foul play. It may have been accidental—or not. She had lost custody of her children, and she took it badly." He finished his coffee. "What's your news?"

"There was a slew of overdoses in New Hampshire. They had 481 opioid deaths last year—the highest rate of fentanyl overdoses in the country. We are seeing something similar here. Then the propofol vial. I think there's a connection."

"How so?"

"Say the New Hampshire dealer moved his business here. George found out. He needed money. He started blackmailing Mr. Overdose. Mr. OD didn't care for the blackmail, so he decided to silence George. He injected George with the propofol he had brought from New Hampshire and nearly killed him." Emma sighed. "Too bad that the nurse is dead!"

"Especially for her." Zagarian took another sip of coffee. "How does one get fentanyl?"

"Melting used patches. You can make it from scratch—the lab equipment is easy to get. The easiest is buying it online. Once you've established your credentials with the supplier, you're all set. There are hundreds of suppliers all over the world. They sell high-purity, uncut fentanyl powder. The dealer cuts it himself."

"Cuts it?"

"Dilutes it. Pure fentanyl is too potent to use. A pinch of it can kill you. You have to dilute it to get a manageable volume for a dose. If you don't do it correctly, some doses will have more fentanyl than others. The users may get more than they can handle. They'll fall asleep. Forever."

"So maybe Mr. OD got the fentanyl online. He cut it and divided it into individual doses, but didn't do it right?"

"Maybe."

"So you're thinking that Mr. OD came from New Hampshire and is somehow connected to the dead nurse."

"Yes."

"So why the propofol? Why not use fentanyl to kill George?"

"Fentanyl takes too long. George would have woken up from the head injury and fought or screamed for help."

"So your Mr. OD has medical knowledge, medical connections, and can access the ED showers. Mr. OD may be working in your ED."

"He might."

"Any ideas?"

"None. I can't believe any of my people would do this."

"Anybody with New Hampshire connections?"

"Carlos and Faith, two of our nurses, came from New Hampshire a few months ago."

"Anybody else?"

"Roy, one of the EMTs, had a cousin there. She died from an OD last summer. Ken, our director, had a cabin in New Hampshire. He vacationed there every summer. Everybody has been to New Hampshire one time or another. By the way, what's happening with Ken's inquest? Any progress?"

"We have no reason to believe that the two are related, at this time."

"Really?"

"Listen, Emma. George was assaulted in the ED during his shift. You are a doctor and the ED director. I have reasons to discuss this case with you. The other one is different. I can't discuss it with you."

"Isn't it too much of a coincidence? Two unrelated deaths happening one week apart on hospital premises?"

"What I suspect and what I can prove are two different things. I'm working on it. That's all I've got for now." He took another sip from his empty coffee cup.

Emma crossed her arms, pretending not to notice.

"Any other New Hampshire connections?" he asked, setting the cup on the side table.

"Ann, one of our docs, does some locums work; she did a stint there last summer."

"That's it?"

Emma shrugged. "I don't know everybody's personal life. Try Jennie, the secretary. She knows everybody and everything."

"Anything else?"

Lips tight, she shook her head no.

"How well do you know Dr. Crump?"

"He's a colleague. We've worked together for years. We don't socialize outside work."

"Did you know that Dr. Crump and George had a big fight the day before George got attacked? Dr. Crump stormed out of the med room so fast that he almost knocked down one of the nurses."

"Who told you?"

Zagarian shrugged.

"That fight may have nothing to do with the assault."

"Dr. Crump said George had made a medication error. He couldn't remember the patient or the details."

"Who'd remember a patient's name a week later? I wouldn't."

"I asked George. He couldn't remember."

"No wonder, after the head injury and all that propofol."

"The propofol was the next day. How far back do people get retrograde amnesia?"

"A few minutes, maybe? But the head injury is another matter altogether."

"I asked him again. He changed his tune. Dr. Crump had apparently gotten mad about a delay in a critical EKG. I say they're both lying."

"I don't think so. Dr. Crump is a decent man," Emma said.

"Does he like money?"

"Who doesn't?" She remembered Kurt's new Audi A7, his gleaming Italian shoes, and his trips to Vegas. *Maybe he likes money more than most.*

"He was in New Hampshire last summer."

"He visited Ken. They were good friends."

"He has a pretty lady friend. She just bought a new car that she can't afford."

Kayla.

Ken was going to demote Kurt...

No. It can't be.

But...

43

EMMA TIED the blue plastic apron tight around her, getting ready for the incoming trauma. Her gloves ripped as she tried to pull them on. She sighed. It was going to be one of those days.

Mondays were always a curse, with way more patients than any other day. Today was also the tail end of a snowstorm. People were coming in like crazy—car accidents, heart attacks from shoveling snow, broken legs from falling off the roof, broken hips after slipping on the ice, kids sleighing into trees, hands filleted by snowblowers.

During the storm, like during the Super Bowl or Thanksgiving dinner, things weren't bad, but the storm was over now.

The team in Trauma 3 looked like a flock of blue Martians in their full protective garb—gloves, hat, booties. They wore tags to recognize each other.

"Pedestrian hit by a car," EMS said. "A hit-and-run."

That was never good. Emma looked at Brenda, who was in charge.

"Any news?"

"A woman. She was hit by a truck. She was unresponsive at the scene, vomited twice, agonal breathing. They are bagging. Probable right femur fracture."

The femur, the largest bone in the body, connecting the hip to the knee, is the hardest to break. That meant high impact, and probably more bad injuries.

"Vitals?"

"OK, they said, except for the tachycardia."

Emma tried to build a mental picture of the patient. *Unresponsive and vomiting! Head injury? Increased intracranial pressure? The broken femur is bad enough by itself, but the kind of force that would break her femur may cause internal injuries and other fractures. Pelvis? Maybe the neck? That could mean paralysis, even death, if the break is high enough to paralyze the diaphragm. The agonal breathing doesn't sound good. This gal is fixing to die. I hate it when they do that!*

"ETA?"

"Five minutes," Brenda said, just as they heard the sirens.

The sirens approached. Emma went to meet them. The two minutes that she stole this way, listening to the EMTs before they landed in the noisy trauma room, gave her a better chance to understand the situation. She won an extra minute to think through her decisions.

Every one of her orders could be a life-or-death sentence for the patient. If she got it wrong, it could be the end of her career.

Every single time, she had to choose the right procedure and order the right medication in the correct dosage for people she'd never seen, before even learning what was wrong with them.

Like now. So many of my friends cracked under pressure and quit. They retired, they moved to urgent care, they became drug reps. I may be the next.

She punched the silver plate to open the door, forgetting everything else but this patient.

Brent, the EMT, opened the door and smiled, recognizing her under the blue garb.

"Hi, Dr. Steele, fifty-two-year-old female hit by a truck. She was unresponsive at the scene; now she's more agitated. She's breathing on her own. Vitals are OK except for tachycardia. She has a right femur deformity. We collared and boarded her, but she started agitating on the way. She vomited twice."

"Did she aspirate?" Boarded and collared was standard procedure for traumas, immobilizing the patient to prevent further injuries. They lay on their back, unable to move or even turn their head. Vomiting was bad. The stomach contents could choke them to death, or at least give them a nasty pneumonia.

"We lifted the board on its side."

Emma nodded.

"Vitals?"

"Blood pressure 95/63, heart rate 123, oxygen sats low 90s."

The heart rate is higher than the blood pressure. That's bad. Plus that blood pressure is too low anyhow. She's bleeding somewhere, probably inside. That broken femur will lose a lot of blood but not enough to make her unstable. I hope she's not bleeding in her brain too; that would explain her agitation. At least she's breathing on her own. For now.

They moved her to the ER stretcher.

"Airway patent. Breathing. Vitals you can read on your own," Emma dictated.

The recorder noted in the trauma sheet.

Emma looked at the bloody face covered in dirt. Left forehead hematoma. A split lip, bleeding. Eyes closed. She tried to pry them open, but the patient resisted. *Good.*

They unbuckled the straps attaching her to the rigid board. The trauma shears came out of many pockets, shredding her wet dirty jacket and pants, then the sweater underneath to expose her.

Emma considered intubating.

Looking iffy. C-collar. She'll need in-line stabilization. Her cheeks are sinking in. No teeth. We'll have a hard time getting a good seal if she needs bagging. Marginal blood pressure. Not just yet.

The left leg looked OK. The right one was in traction, pulled away from her body in a Hare splint. *Looks like a medieval torture device. Must feel like one too.* Her chest was raising symmetrically with every breath. The abdomen looked distended. Emma grabbed the pelvic bones, pushing them together. They didn't move. *No instability.* She pinched her toenails, then her thumbs, checking for sensation and strength. She pulled away. *Good.* She opened her C-collar to inspect the neck, then closed it back, protecting the spine. She listened to the lungs, then palpated her abdomen. The woman gave a bloodcurdling scream.

Emma looked up. Kayla, in the door, was waiting for orders.

"Hold the scanner and get me the surgeon."

"What are you scanning?"

"Everything. Head, neck, chest, abdomen, and pelvis. Something bad's happening, and she's too out of it to show us what. I need her history, allergies, and meds. Is she on any blood thinners?"

"I'm on it," Brenda said.

"What does she have for IV access?"

"An 18 in the left AC and a 20 in the right by EMT," Judy said.

"She'll need blood. Can you get in a 16?" The smaller the number, the larger the needle in the IV world; larger needles meant faster treatment, faster fluids, and blood—all essential for someone on the edge to stay alive.

Judy nodded.

"Blood pressure dropping."

Emma glanced at the monitor.

Dropping indeed. 87/65. Heart rate climbing to compensate. Thank God she's breathing on her own; if I had to intubate her right now, I'd kill her. "IV fluids under pressure, please. Two liters. Has the blood arrived?"

"O negative here," said the blood-bank kid. He was standing in the corner with his cooler, keeping out of the way. He looked ready for a picnic, but this was no picnic. *This is death knocking. Not on my watch.*

"Let's give two units. We sent blood for type and cross and the rest of the trauma panel, yes?"

"Yes," three voices answered.

She rechecked the lungs. *Still OK.* They log-rolled her to her left, checking her spine. Emma walked her gloved fingers over each vertebra, looking for step-ups or pain, indicative of a fracture. There was none. She considered doing a rectal exam, then decided against it. *It won't change the management; she's off to the scanner no matter what. There's no time to waste.* She was ready to roll her back when something blue on the left scapula caught her attention. She brushed the dirt away.

Though marred by dry blood, the intricate blue shape was clear.

A blue spider.

44

"CT SCAN IS READY," Kayla said.

The blood pressure is above 90; the pulse is better. She's going in the right direction. She's breathing. Getting blood. She calmed down. The surgeon is on his way; he'll want the CT scan before taking her to the OR. She's as good as she's going to get. I'd better scan her before she crashes.

"Let's go."

If she crashes in the CT scan, I'm screwed. That's a sucky place to run a code—no space, no equipment, not enough staff. If I don't send her and she gets worse, as I know she will, I've missed the opportunity to scan her before opening her on the OR table. Damned if you do, damned if you don't. Emma shrugged and joined the CT procession. *I'd better be there if things turn bad. The others look like they'll stay alive for now.*

The surgeon on call, Dr. Brody, a thick man of few nice words, met them at the scanner.

She told him the story. He didn't look pleased.

"Did you give her blood?"

"She's getting her second unit."

"Did you do a rectal?"

"No. I didn't think she needed one."

Dr. Brody frowned. "Didn't they teach you in medical school, if you ever went to medical school, that the only two reasons to not perform a rectal in a trauma victim are the patient not having a rectum or the surgeon not having a finger?"

"Well, I'm not a surgeon. You are. Feel free to do the rectal."

He frowned deeper. "You're sure she didn't need a chest tube before sticking her in the scanner?

"As sure as I get."

"Is she on any blood thinners?"

"Not that we know of."

"You don't know much about her, do you?"

"I know more than you do. She's been here for all of 20 minutes. We got access, we resuscitated her, and we got her in the scanner. Oh, and we gave her TXA."

"TXA? Tranexamic acid? Why?"

"So that she doesn't bleed out before you take her to the OR." Emma had had enough of being treated like she didn't know what she was doing. "Read the literature. It's recommended immediately in trauma with serious blood loss."

"Who said I'm taking her to the OR?"

"I did. Let me know if you don't."

"Hmm."

"Can you take it from here? There's no point for both of us staying with her in the scanner."

"Yep."

"Thank you."

After the CT, the patient went straight to the OR. Emma wondered how she did. She wanted to call and find out, but she got busy and forgot. When the surgeon called her, four hours later, it felt like it had happened weeks ago.

"She's doing OK. She'll pull through."

"Wonderful. Thank you so much for coming!"

"Not like I had a choice."

What a charmer! "Thank you anyhow."

As she was ready to hang up, he said, "You're welcome. You did a good job down there. Half an hour longer and she'd have bled to death. She had a liver laceration and a tear in the vena cava. Barely made it."

"Thanks again." Emma hung up, fighting to hold her tears. Dealing with kindness was not her thing. She wasn't used to it. Pressure and insults—that, she was used to.

"She made it." Her nurses stared at her, not understanding. It had been many patients ago.

"Our trauma this morning. The hit-and-run. Dr. Brody said she'll pull through."

They smiled. Things like this made up for being harassed, peed on, sworn at, and abused every shift.

"Good job, team! I'm proud of you!"

"We're proud of you, Dr. Steele. She was lucky to have you."

45

THAT'S NO GOOD. The toddler in Room 4 was sitting upright on the stretcher. He looked like the bucolic angels on chocolate boxes, with his curly hair and blue eyes, but he was in trouble.

His chest moved way too fast at sixty breaths a minute. His nostrils flared like a bunny's, and his little potbelly pulled in with every breath. *Subcostal retractions; he's struggling to breathe. His oxygen saturation's OK, but then it always is, until they crash. There are almost no breath sounds; he isn't moving much air.*

"Has he done this before?"

The young mother—way too young—was holding another baby in her arms. Her eyes were wide with fear. She nodded, "But never this bad."

"Did they tell you he has asthma?"

"They said something like reductive..."

"Reactive airway disease." The mother nodded again. That was the code word for asthma in young kids.

"Do you have a nebulizer machine at home?"

"Yes, but I ran out of the vials yesterday."

"So, no treatments today?"

The woman shook her head.

Good. A few treatments and some steroids, and he might turn around. Faith, his nurse, brought in the nebulizer—a clear plastic pipe connected to oxygen, releasing a white mist of medicine. She handed it to Mom, who tried to direct the mist toward the toddler while holding her baby.

Not even close.

No good.

"Faith, please administer the Duoneb yourself; then get me a new set of vitals."

She left the room to find the vice president of medical affairs waiting for her.

"You have a moment?"

"Sure."

They walked into the nearest empty room.

"How are you?"

"I'm OK. What's up?"

"We have a complaint."

"About me?"

"About the ED. We were cited for an EMTALA violation."

Horrific. EMTALA, the Emergency Medical Treatment and Labor Act, mandated hospitals and doctors to care for sick patients regardless of their ability to pay, making it illegal to transfer patients before stabilizing them. Being found guilty of an EMTALA could cut off the hospital from Medicaid and Medicare. That meant bankruptcy.

"How so?"

"That sick kid you transferred the other night?"

"Yes."

"He died yesterday. I looked at your documentation. I didn't find much."

"I was taking care of him; I didn't have time to document."

"You need to flesh out your documentation. If they find us in violation, we're toast."

"I understand."

That case broke her heart. She'd been wondering day and night if there was anything more she could have done. She had run the case through her mind a hundred times. Still, she hadn't found anything that she wished she could change, but that didn't make her feel any better. The kid was dead. She had failed to save him. And now this EMTALA crap. *My job is on the line. If they find me guilty, I can get a $100,000 fine, and fines aren't covered by my malpractice. I don't have the money. If I lose my job, I have no way to get it. I'm screwed.*

She shrugged. This could wait. She went back to Room 4. The kid looked better, his breathing now improved. He was still retracting, but he paid more attention to the world around him and wheezed like a locomotive. *Great—he's moving some air. Another couple of treatments and he may be going home.* Mom, her eyelids heavy now that the danger seemed past, smiled.

Emma stepped out to find Dr. Umber waiting.

"Just letting you know that I can't work next month."

"How come?"

"A family emergency."

"A family emergency next month, and you know about it now?"

"Look, I'm trying to be polite about it. I thought I'd let you know ahead of time."

He's supposed to work in a couple of weeks, a string of three nights. That'll be a bitch to cover. Nobody wants to work nights. Still, better to know about it now than get called when he doesn't show up for his shift.

I wonder what's up.

46

Kayla put on the last touch of lipstick and checked her watch. *It's time.* She grabbed her overnight bag, looked around to make sure she hadn't forgotten anything, and opened the door. Dick was waiting.

He had invited her for a weekend of skiing, wine, and adult conversation. She'd felt guilty about leaving Eden, but his friend Jake had invited him for a sleepover. He'd been ecstatic.

Dick stepped out to open the car door for her. He kissed her softly and helped her in, making her feel like a princess.

The old inn was enchanting. White candles standing in silver candlesticks played lights and shadows over the melt-in-your-mouth broiled scallops and gleaming sweet lobster. Crystal glasses fractured the light into rainbows. Soft guitar music set the romantic mood.

They ate the luxurious food, drank too much buttery French wine, and talked.

"Is Eden's father involved in his life?"

"He's deployed, so he's seldom here. He sends him Christmas gifts. They only meet a couple times a year."

"It must be hard to be a single mother."

"It's gotten easier as he's gotten older. He's a good kid."

"He is. He's handsome and smart."

"You have kids?"

"Two."

"How old?"

"Seven. Twins."

"Boys or girls?"

"One of each."

"Do you spend time with them?"

"Not much, with my crazy schedule. They live with their mother. We Skype. In January I took them skiing in Colorado. We had a great time. Soon enough they'll ditch me for their friends."

Kayla laughed.

"I love your laugh." He caressed the edge of her hand with his finger. "It's like a light coming on inside you."

She laughed again.

"I love everything about you, Kayla," he said, looking deep in her eyes.

Kayla blushed and took another sip of wine. "Nice wine," she said.

"It's a grand cru. I love white burgundy. It's smooth and buttery like nothing else. Except..." he said, and kissed her. "It tastes even better from you."

She laughed again, half embarrassed, half flattered, drunk all the way with wine and romance.

Dessert came covered by a silver cloche. It wasn't food. It was a tiny golden box tied with a silver ribbon. The diamond inside sparkled and flashed with fiery lights, putting the candles to shame. Kayla's heart melted.

He put it on her finger.

"It's beautiful!"

"Not as beautiful as you," he said, kissing her. He took her hand and led her upstairs to the room under the eaves. There was no number, just a plaque: "The Princess Suite." He picked her up and carried her in. Kayla felt like a princess. He laid her on the bearskin in front of the fireplace.

The burning logs crackled and hissed as he undressed her, kissing every inch of her. He kissed her mouth. His tongue tasted like pepper and honey and wine. He kissed her left eye, then slid to her left temple. He gently bit her earlobe; then his lips slid down the side of her neck to her breasts, and down to her navel, and lower still. He reached the place between her legs, which was waiting for him. He kissed it and blew on it. She shivered. His tongue found it. She remembered no more.

Ages later, they lay embraced on the bearskin, watching the fire. He caressed her, his nimble fingers playing havoc with her senses.

"Let's go to Mexico. You, me, and Eden," he said.

"And just leave everything behind?"

"Why not? Life's too short to miss the good times. We'll surf, we'll lie on the beach drinking margaritas, and we'll ride horses in the ocean."

"I don't know how to ride a horse."

"You'll learn, my dear. You'll learn that, and many other things."

She wondered what that meant, but he started kissing her again, and she forgot.

By the time she remembered, it was too late to ask. She was back home, looking at the selfie she'd taken of them both on the bearskin.

47

SPIDER MAN STAYED DEAD. Just another homeless person found dead in the snow. His damaged body told about a rough life. His scarred veins witnessed a long love affair with drugs. He was going to be a coroner's case, but the chances of finding anything were slim.

Emma talked to the policeman who'd come to the ED to investigate. She told him about the man with the spider tattoo who'd been looking for Ken.

He didn't care.

He's not gonna look into it.

I will.

She got spider man's name, address, and phone number from the records. She called. No answer. A robot asked her to leave a message. She hung up.

She drove to his place downtown. The decrepit house was one step away from being boarded up. Silent and dark. Snow piled on the doorstep, untouched after the last storm. She knocked. No answer. She tried the door. It was locked, but the hinges were falling out of the rotten wood. One good shove would get it open. *I shouldn't go in. I should call Zagarian.*

She remembered the last time they met. She'd been so angry that she'd almost thrown him out. She clenched her teeth and got out her phone. Dead battery.

She headed to her car.

It's the reasonable thing to do. There's nothing urgent about this. The guy's chilling at the morgue. Not going anywhere. I'll charge my phone. I'll call Zagarian.

She took two steps and froze.

What if somebody finds out he's dead and comes to check his place and remove any evidence? What if they know already? What if they're on their way? By the time police arrive, with their mandate and paperwork—IF they do—everything will be long gone.

She went back. She shivered.

What if they're already here, waiting? That's stupid; nobody knows I'm here. Nobody opened that door since yesterday, at least. But the windows...

She kicked the door, hard. It cracked open like a gunshot, letting out darkness.

Emma slid in. She looked for the light switch. She found it.

No light.

She took out her flashlight. The shard of light split the darkness. Scattered glimmers reflected on the snowflakes following her in. The room was almost empty. A mattress. A table. Two chairs. A woodstove. A door.

She pulled the door closed behind her. The room got darker.

It was cold.

She opened the other door. A bathroom. Filthy. Empty but for a stack of syringes and needles in a metal box.

The lonely life of a drug addict.

The tears came out of nowhere. Tears for the lonely, miserable life of this man who must have been somebody's son, somebody's lover. *He's nobody now. Nothing.*

Why was he looking for Ken? Who was he? Did he really have a son?

She searched the place.

I shouldn't be here. If they come, I'll tell them I'm looking for some info on his family so that we can contact them about his death.

She was fast and quiet. She held the flashlight in her mouth to keep her hands free. *Nothing. Nothing in the table drawer, nothing under the mattress, nothing in between the old clothes that served as sheets.*

She heard crepitus as she grabbed the pillow. She palpated it gently, like she would a baby's belly. Nothing. She was about to put it back when she saw the sliver of paper coming out of a hole. She pulled it out. Feathers fell gently on the dirty floor. The yellow piece of paper, ripped from a notebook, was wrinkled. The writing was large, irregular, and childish.

The words were not.

SPIDER

My last will
I leave everything I own to my ex-wife Jessy.
I'm sorry I died without saying I'm sorry.
I was no good. You were right to ditch me.
Love you still and always.
Look inside the oak tree.
Love you.
Spy."

48

TAYLOR WAS ABOUT to lose it. Her eyes were burning, and she was choking on the knot in her throat. *Three days now and not a single call. Why? Where is he?*

Sick with worry, she bit her fingernails to the quick. She had called a hundred times. No answer. She had left messages.

She was reading *The Chamber of Secrets* for the fourth time as the phone rang. Her heart burst.

It's him.

"Hello, baby. How did it go?" His low, soothing voice was a caress.

"It went great. You were right. She swallowed it like candy."

"She's going to do it?"

"She said she would."

"Good girl!"

Taylor felt proud. She thought it wasn't going to be easy to fool her mother, but he was right. She had swallowed the rape story, hook, line, and sinker. It was a good story too; she had found it on the Internet. It worked like a charm, except that her mother had been hell-bent on reporting the rape. Taylor acted despondent. She cried, pleaded, threw herself on the floor. "It would kill me to go through the details once more, Mother."

Emma had relented, but Taylor wondered if she'd report it anyhow. *Hopefully not. She promised. She's always gung-ho about keeping her word. Either way, she's going to help with the abortion.*

"When?" he asked.

"Next week. I'll fly back on Monday."

"I miss you," he said.

Her heart softened. She had never loved anybody like she loved him.

"I miss you too. I miss your hands. The scent of your skin. The taste of your kiss."

They had met a few months ago at the ER Halloween party. Her mother had dragged her along. She didn't want to go, but Katie told her that the ER Halloween party was the best in town. DJ, the best costumes, prize drawings.

She got bored to death. All the kids were younger. There was nobody to talk to.

She walked outside. The garden was empty but for a lone smoker. She bummed a cigarette. They talked. He was handsome and funny. He liked her.

He offered her a pill.

"Put it under your tongue."

"Will it make me crazy?"

"No. It will make you feel good, really good."

It did. The sun was shining inside her. Her thoughts became pink and blue. Her weightless body flew at warp speed through a twisting rainbow of colors. She'd never felt better. She cried when she landed.

He kissed her and asked for her phone number.

She asked for his.

He smiled. He'd just lost his phone and needed to get a new one.

He gave her some wonder pills.

"Make sure you're alone for at least an hour before you take them. Never take more than one!"

He'd called a few days later. She had run out of pills. They went to a cozy inn. They drank wine and took pills. His mouth made love to her. That was even better than the pills.

The time after that he made love to her. It hurt so good! She decided that she loved him and she was going to keep him.

He gave her some extra pills for her friends. She wanted to keep them for herself.

"Don't worry, we have plenty more," he said. "Be nice to your friends."

She gave them to her friends, then gave them a few more.

Next time they wanted some, the pills were no longer free. "Ten dollars each," he said. Hers were free. He loved her. He wanted her to feel good.

He was so proud of her when she brought the money.

The pregnancy was a surprise. They had always used condoms, unless they were having oral sex. She started feeling funny. She bought a test. It was positive.

He wasn't pleased.

She wanted to keep the baby. She loved him—she loved his baby.

He disagreed. "The kid's going to be a monster, after all those drugs," he said. "It's going to have two heads, or hands growing out of its shoulders."

He showed her pictures. She cried. She vomited. Heartbroken, she finally agreed to abort, but she needed parental consent.

"I'll take you to your Grandma for a few days," he said. "We'll let your parents stew a little. When they find you, they'll be so happy that they'll do anything you ask. Plus, you won't have to go to school!"

"But I'll miss you!"

"I'll miss you too, baby, but it's only for a few days."

Driving to Georgia was fun. They spent the night at a hotel on the way. They drank champagne, took pills, and made love like never before. He dropped her off at Grandma's door.

A few days later she called Victor. He was so happy that she felt guilty. She got over it.

They didn't even scold her. Still, they didn't want her to get an abortion. They wanted to know who the father was. She couldn't come up with a name. She told Emma the rape story. That worked.

Only a few days now.

Her heart sang.

49

IT WAS TUESDAY, "THE DAY," as Taylor called it. Emma had cold feet.

Biting her lower lip to focus better, Taylor was putting on mascara. *Why does she need mascara to have an abortion? For confidence maybe. Like I put on lipstick before a trauma code. Whatever it is, I hope it helps.*

Emma checked her phone for work emergencies. None. She finished her third coffee. She looked at Taylor. She was pale, fragile, and unafraid.

"Are you sure you want to go through with this?"

"*Yes*. I've told you a hundred times."

"You could stay with Margret; then you could give the baby up for adoption. You could keep in touch with her, if you wanted. You could see her grow."

"See her grow?" Taylor turned, her eyes shooting arrows at Emma. "I don't wanna see her grow. And how do you know it's a girl?"

"Well, see him grow then. The baby, whatever it is."

"It's not gonna be a baby; it's gonna be a monster after

the drugs I took. It won't have arms or legs. It will be a giant toad. I've seen the pictures."

"What pictures?"

"The pictures of the monsters born to druggie mothers."

"Well, it depends on the drugs and how much and how often and..."

"No!" Taylor stormed out, slamming the door.

I wish I could have wine rather than coffee.

She didn't much care about her hypothetical grandchild —she'd been a lousy mother, she wasn't going to be any better as a grandmother—but she was worried about Taylor.

One day she'll realize that she expunged her child. She'll never forgive herself. Abortion has no recourse. Adoption would give her time to think things through.

They drove to the ferry where Victor was waiting and moved into his car.

"Taylor, are you sure?" Victor asked.

"Don't start!" Taylor spitted out. "Don't even go there!"

"But if the baby..."

"I told you, don't go there. I've already had a lecture this morning, thank you very much, not to mention all those I've had over the last few weeks! I've made my decision." She turned her attention to her cell phone. She was done.

Victor sighed.

What the hell did we do to deserve this? We loved her, we cared for her, we bought her the best of everything. True, I never had time for her. Same with Victor. He got her the best bike, the newest phone—but he left her for his new family. We both failed her.

At the hospital, Victor and Emma sat in the waiting room after a nurse took Taylor. Victor read an old magazine. He held it upside down, but he didn't seem to notice.

"Have you been praying?" Emma asked.

"Yes, out of habit. I no longer know what I believe in."

"What have you been praying for?"

"I've prayed for her future and for her to get enlighten-ment to make the right decision, but mostly I've been asking for forgiveness."

"For what?"

"For what I did to her when I left. For what I did to you."

"You did what you had to do. Amber was pregnant. You felt that it was your responsibility to care for her and your child."

"Yes. I also knew that you'd take care of yourself and Taylor while Amber... She's not strong like you; she needs a man."

"I needed you."

"No, you didn't. That was part of the problem. You didn't need me. You didn't really need anyone. You still don't." He took off his glasses and started cleaning them with his shirt. "I think that's why I got involved with Amber. She was vulnerable. She needed somebody to take care of her. I needed to have somebody to care for, somebody to need me."

Emma wanted to tell him that Taylor needed him and that she did too, but what was the point? He was miserable enough. They waited in silence for what seemed like years.

A nurse wheeled Taylor in. She was pale and tight-lipped.

"Let's go."

"How do you feel?"

"Better."

They drove back in silence. Emma felt better too. *It's over. No more "what if" and "how" and "maybe." We can finally move on.*

50

Sitting in her office, Emma was drowning in papers. It was reappointment time. She had to review all the personnel files. Kurt's file looked good. She put it away and got Umber's. He looked good on paper. He even looked good in person. His second reference was from a small hospital in New Hampshire. Something about it bothered her. She Googled it. Winston, New Hampshire, fifty miles from Concord. Coincidence? She called the director, Dr. Slim. He didn't say much.

"He was fine. Competent, fast, a bit of a showoff. No professional issues."

"Anything with the patients or the staff?"

"No," he eventually said.

He's lying. He's afraid of being sued. The darn lawyers make us all paranoid.

"Please tell me! I need to know. This is just between the two of us."

"Well, if anything, he was too friendly."

"The girls?"

"Yes, there were issues with the nurses. Two of them got into a fight. I had to fire one."

Emma remembered the nurse who'd been fired and then died.

"I thought that was for drugs," she said, throwing a dart in the dark.

"Well, yes, that was part of it too. Joy had some issues."

"What happened to her?"

"She died of a drug overdose. I think she couldn't stand the thought that they had taken away her kids."

"Was she involved with Dr. Umber?"

"She was. There were others. Umber's a good doctor, but he just can't keep it zipped. I've never had more trouble with any locum."

Emma thanked him and hung up. She sat at her desk, thinking. *It's Umber. Everything is falling into place; it must be him.*

She called Zagarian. His phone sent her directly to his voice mail.

Umber must have brought the propofol from New Hampshire. He'd been involved with the nurse who signed it out. He attacked George. He was working a shift that day. He left his area for a few minutes to meet George in the shower room. George wanted more money. Umber assaulted him, injected him with propofol, and then left him there to die. He went back to his patients like nothing happened. Somebody found George. They brought him to the ED and gave him to Umber! No wonder Umber was rattled!

But why didn't he let him die?

He couldn't! All eyes were on them. Every member of the staff was watching George like a hawk. Police came. Umber couldn't take the risk. He pretended to save George's life to shake any possible suspicion. He could do nothing else. He thought George would die anyhow.

How about Ken? Did he kill Ken? Why?

Umber wouldn't cut Ken's throat. He'd find a more elegant way. Like getting the Spider to do his dirty work.

Emma had wanted to give Zagarian the Spider's will, but she couldn't explain how she got it. She couldn't tell him she broke into his house. Still, she wasn't sorry. She was sure he was connected to Ken's death. She'd tried to find Spider's ex-wife. She was listed in his chart as his next of kin, but the phone was disconnected and there was no address. *Dead end.*

She called Zagarian.

"There's this homeless guy with a spider tattoo who was looking for Ken. He ended up dead in the snow a few days later. He's a coroner's case. His ex-wife is his next of kin. She may have some information about Ken's death if we could find her."

"Why should she?"

Emma had hemmed and hawed. "I can't tell you. But I know she's got some of his stuff. In an oak tree." *How stupid does that sound?!*

"We'll look for her. Emma, do me a favor?"

"Yes?"

"Stay out of trouble. Whatever you did, don't do it again. Whatever you found, put it back. Whoever you spoke to, don't do it again. There's a killer on the loose, and you're no match for him. He's gonna chew you up and spit you out before you can say Merry Christmas. Keep out of it, please!"

Emma hung up.

She hadn't heard from him since.

I know it's Umber.

51

SHE PICKED up her white coat. *Boy, is it heavy! I have to throw away some of the crap in the pockets. No wonder my shoulders hurt!*

She put it on over her street clothes and walked down to the ED. The place was its usual shade of crazy, one step short of frantic. Umber was in Trauma 2, dressed in full sterile garb—coat, hat, shield, booties—putting in a central line. He looked like he was having trouble finding the subclavian. He asked the nurse to reposition the patient and started over.

He's gonna be at it at least another ten minutes. She looked at her watch, then speed-walked to the doctor's lounge. She punched in the code, walked in, and closed the door behind her.

His bag, an expensive Italian burgundy leather affair, looked out of place on the cheap green vinyl sofa. It was heavy.

She opened it: a brand new little EMRA guide to antibiotics, a heavy *Emergency Medicine Procedures* book that had seen better days, a *Rolling Stone* magazine, a deodorant, a toothbrush, a tube of Sensodyne, a pair of socks.

What the hell am I even looking for? Two brown medicine bottles, unlabeled, half full. She opened them. One had twenty-two white oblong tablets. The other had twenty-seven round pink pills.

What are they? I should take them with me. Shit, I left my fingerprints all over them. I should have worn gloves, darn it! Too late now.

She took two tablets out of each bottle, dropped them in her chest pocket, wiped the bottles with the tails of her white coat, and placed them back in the bag. *If I wiped away my prints I also wiped his, so they're no longer on the bottles. More likely I left mine everywhere. Stupid! Too late to worry about that now.*

She checked her watch. *Eight minutes. I need to get the hell out of here.* She looked around. His red ski jacket was hanging in the corner.

She looked through the pockets. *Wallet. Credit cards in his name. Healthcare ID. Cash: a couple of hundreds, a few twenties, a lot of tens. Passport.* She opened it to check it—*in his name, has his picture, it looks valid.* She put it back. *Cell phone, tissues, coins, condoms, a power bar, matches, a brown envelope.* She opened it. *Pictures.*

She went through them: *snow-capped mountains, ski slopes, a boat, a vineyard—it's twelve minutes now—more trees covered in snow, a naked girl, a car... The girl!*

She went back.

Taylor, naked, smiled at her from the picture.

The door opened.

52

UMBER STEPPED in and closed the door.

"I knew I shouldn't have taken that with me," he said, sitting in the desk chair and rolling it in front of the door. "Taylor insisted. She said she wanted me to remember her by it."

Emma stood frozen, looking at him.

"So, what are you going to do?"

She was angry. She was so angry that her brain was on fire and she couldn't think straight. She wanted to cry and she wanted to scream, and more than anything she wanted to hurt him. Bad.

Thankfully, a lifetime with the crazy had taught her that letting your anger take hold of you made you a loser. She took a deep breath and closed her fury in a small dark corner of her brain. She'd get it out later.

"About what?"

"About that." He nodded to the picture.

"Nothing, I think. Too late to do anything now. I hope you gave her a good experience. The first time is important, especially for a girl. I want her to like sex. It's a joyful thing."

"Really?"

No, not really, but she wasn't going to tell him that.

"I will tell the police about your drug dealing though, Mr. OD. That should put you away for a while."

He laughed. "No, you won't."

"Why not?"

"I have your Taylor. In every way."

"How so?"

"Who do you think did the selling for me? Who do you think got her friends hooked and collected the money?"

"Who?" She smiled, feeling her sweat freezing on her back. *That can't be true. Yes, it can.*

"Taylor. If I fall, she falls. She was the dealer, really; I just procured the merchandise for her. How do you think she'll fare in jail?" Umber asked.

"She'll have a rough time, I guess. No mascara, no cell phone..."

Emma took the other seat and sat, facing him. She crossed her legs casually and put her hands in her pockets. The scalpel was there, in the right pocket, where it belonged. In the ED, one never knows when there's something needing cutting.

She checked her other pocket. Her eye drops were there. So was the bottle of hemocult developer, the concentrated alcohol drops used to test for rectal bleeding. She'd learned the hard way that you should never confuse the two. One night she'd dripped one drop of hemocult in her eye. She couldn't open it for a week. *It's pure alcohol; you'd be better off drinking it then putting it in your eye.*

She rearranged her stethoscope, a Littmann Master Cardiology III, around her neck. It was good and heavy. It made a good weapon. Since Ken's death she'd been practicing in her basement. She'd learned to swing it like a pro.

She could hit something six feet away with a good flick of her wrist.

She leaned back, uncrossed her feet, and smiled politely. "On the other hand, she could finish high school without skipping classes. She'd get an actual education."

"Really? Would you really do that to your daughter?"

"Me? Absolutely not. I would never do anything bad to my daughter. You did. By the way, is the baby yours?"

"What did she tell you?"

"You know what she told me; you taught her." Emma smiled. "So. Is the baby yours?"

"Probably."

"Very nice. With you and Taylor as parents, it should be handsome and smart."

"You told her you'll help her get an abortion."

"Sure I did. That was then. This is now. I can deal with a drug dealer as a son-in-law. I can even care for the baby as long as you're both in jail, or I can hire somebody to do it. Would you prefer a little girl or a little boy?"

His face got white and narrow as the business end of an axe.

"You're bluffing. You'd never ever do this to your daughter."

She smiled.

"You have no proof."

"Oh, but I do. The bottles in your bag. Taylor's statements. Oh, and that nurse in New Hampshire? Joy? She left a letter."

"No she didn't. You're full of shit. There was no letter."

"You checked then?"

He turned dark and stood just as the speakers blurted: "Dr. Umber to Room 3."

He leaped toward her.

It was time. She let her anger out of its dark corner. It gave her wings.

His first punch knocked over her chair, but she'd already jumped on her feet. She stepped sideways. His weight took him past her into the wall. She grabbed the stethoscope and spun it above her head. He charged again, his fists ready to pummel her. The stethoscope got him just below his left eye. The zygomatic bone cracked.

He screamed. He stumbled but didn't fall. He was too close for the stethoscope now. She dropped it. She grabbed her scalpel with her right hand. She opened it with her thumb as she was falling backward under his weight. They fell, him on top. The speakers screamed again: "Dr. Umber to Room 3." *He won't make it.*

His weight pinned her pelvis to the ground. His right hand reached for her throat. She lifted the scalpel to open his carotids. *That will make a bloody mess. I really want him in jail.* She went for his right hand instead. She sliced cleanly through the wrist. He roared. *I got him. Good.*

She dropped the scalpel, now slippery with blood. He grabbed her throat with his other hand. He squeezed. He choked her. She twisted under him. Her left hand grabbed the hemocult bottle she'd uncapped as they were talking. She squeezed it in his eyes. She missed.

"Dr. Umber to Room 3," the speakers pleaded, desperate now. *I hope somebody'll take care of Room 3.*

She squeezed the bottle again. His bloodcurdling scream told her she got him. She felt a sting in her right thigh as she pushed him off. She squeezed out from under him. She stood and opened the door. Covered in blood, he was rubbing his eyes with his good hand. She stepped out and closed the door.

The world went dark.

53

EMMA OPENED HER EYES. Suspended ceiling. The recessed lights were off. She tried to sit up. She couldn't. Her right arm didn't move. Neither did the left.

A stroke?

She tried the legs. They worked. She turned her head right. A wall. She turned it left. A door. Closed. Light outside. Noise. ED noise. She opened and closed her fists— both working. Shoulders too. Wrists hurt.

Not a stroke. Then what?

She lifted her head and looked at herself. She was lying on a stretcher, dressed in blue paper scrubs, the uniform of the mental health patients. Her wrists and her ankles were in soft restraints. She could see the corner of the nursing desk, so she knew that she was in Room 6, one of the three rooms for mental health patients.

She was tied down in her own ED.

I'm a mental health patient?!

The door opened. Umber came in.

"How are you doing?"

"Excellent. Resting. You?"

"Great." *He's lying.* He had a bump the size of a goose egg over his left ear. His eyes were too swollen to tell the color. His right hand was splinted and bandaged, sitting in a sling. *I did a good job.* Then she remembered that she was cuffed to the stretcher and felt less sure.

"Police were here. I told them that you had a psychotic break when you found out that I was dating your daughter. You attacked me and tried to kill me. Fortunately, I happened to have a sedative with me. That saved my life."

"Nicely done," she nodded. *So that's what that sharp pain was. I should have thought about it. I didn't. Umber one, Emma zero.*

"Ketamine?"

Umber smiled and nodded. "You really are smart, for a woman. I like that. I have a deal for you. I'll say that you were so mad with grief for your daughter that you attacked me, but I won't press charges as long as you don't mention the drugs. You can't prove it anyhow.

"How about the two bottles in your bag? And how about Taylor?"

"The bottles are now in the pockets of your white coat. They have your fingerprints all over them. Only yours. I always handle them with gloves. For all that I know, you may be the drug dealer, Dr. Steele. As for Taylor, who do you think she's gonna support?"

Emma had lost hope for her relationship with Taylor long ago. Taylor's latest lies were further proof that she'd be a fool to trust her. *Taylor will never support me against Dick. He won.*

He'd won her daughter. He'd soiled her reputation. He had destroyed just about everything she cared about. She despised him.

"You are smart. Very smart in fact. You are smooth,

charming, and attractive. You play people. You turn the heads of innocent girls. You get them addicted and make them your slaves. Does that make you feel good?"

"It does. I've never felt better in my entire life."

He pulled the chair closer to the head of the bed. He sat crossing his right leg over his left knee to rest his splinted arm on top of it. His face would have made Picasso proud, but his mood was elated. His words were coming out fast and furious.

"I hate you. I hate people like you, who think they are better than me. You called me a licensed drug peddler, remember? Told me that I should act like a doctor. Well, let me tell you something, doctor. My mother was an addict. I never knew my father. I grew up in the streets. I never knew when my next meal was coming.

"At nine, I knew how to buy and sell. She'd send me out to get her fix. I got to see things no child should see and withstand things no child should ever withstand. I had to do anything—*anything*—to get her fix. Once she got it, she was grateful and loving. I was her lovely little boy. Until the next morning. She'd wake up shivering and crazy. She'd send me out for more.

"Day after day after day, that's what my childhood was, selling myself to help my mother. One day she didn't wake up. She was cold when I tried to wake her up. They took her to the morgue, and they put me in foster care. That was fun too, house after house of lowlifes using me as free labor and as an opportunity to vent their bile against those smarter than them, literate and hardworking.

"I went through high school, college, and medical school using the skills I'd learned as a child. It felt good to stick it to those who'd enjoyed hurting me.

"Now I'm rich, strong, and free. I can get anything and

anyone I want. That makes me feel good, really good. It pleases me to no end to have you down, tied down like a nutcase in your own department. No matter what happens, you'll be too embarrassed to ever set foot in here again. I made that happen.

"Yes, I'm very pleased. I got you down, and I'll destroy you. In fact, you'll destroy yourself; you are well on the way to doing that. I couldn't do as good a job as you have in a hundred years."

"How about statutory rape?"

"You should read the law, Doctor. That's not an issue at Taylor's age. Moreover, who'll complain? You, who tried to kill me and barely failed? Let me be!" he said, laughing. "You're toast, Dr. Steele. You daughter hates you, your career is finished, you may even go to jail for drug trafficking. Wouldn't that be fun!

"I'll take care of Taylor, you know. She'll go into the business and learn. She's really good at it. Education doesn't mean crap to her; she doesn't care about it. But selling? She loves it! You'll be proud of her when you get out of jail— what will they give you for assault and attempted murder? Ten years? Twenty? You'll lose your license and any friends you've got left. You could work at McDonald's—if they take convicts. Do you know how to flip a burger?"

"Not really. I'd rather cook inside. You?"

"Well, you'll get to practice during your jail days. I heard they teach inmates all sorts of skills."

He turned to the door.

"Why did you kill Ken?"

"I didn't."

"You got your Spider to do it."

"Smart girl."

"Why?"

"He ditched me. I'd just built a network to replace New Hampshire; now I had to move again. Bad for business, you know."

"Did you kill the Spider too?"

"Not me. He overdosed. I just gave him the fentanyl. Pure fentanyl."

"Why?"

"He outlived his usefulness. He was a liability."

"And George?"

"He was too greedy."

"You are the essence of evil!"

"What a compliment. Thank you!"

54

EMMA HATED HIM. She hated him more than she'd ever hated anyone. He was the worst human being she'd ever seen. She was going to destroy him.

Somehow.

What if I go to jail?

It can't be any worse than this, for fuck's sake. I've wasted my whole life. I've been playing a part, trying to be the person the others wanted me to be instead of who I really am.

First, Mother. I tried to be the perfect daughter to please her. But there was no pleasing her. She could give Marquis de Sade a run for his money.

Then Victor. I tried to be the woman he wanted, to make him love me and keep me. Then Amber came, and I was history.

Then Taylor. I was her mother. She had to love me and need me. Hah! If I drowned in the back yard, she'd be pissed that I fouled the pool.

I've never been essential to anybody.

Nobody gave a shit about her. Not even herself.

She lay alone in the dark, listening to the noises. Speakers, alarms, stretchers rolling along the hallways. The hushed voices of the nurses, her friends, only feet away.

Nobody came.

Her own people, her work family, closer than her real one, ignored her.

She was alone.

There was only one person left to care for.

Not Taylor, the bane of her existence since the day she was born; nor Victor, who'd left her; nor her mother, who screwed up her brain into the mess she was.

It was her, Emma.

She did her best. She failed.

The world could take care of itself.

It was time to put Emma first.

Tied to the stretcher, accused of a crime she didn't commit, she was in peace. The weight of the world fell off her shoulders—tomorrow's shift, Umber, Taylor, EMTALA. Defeated, tied down, humiliated in front of her beloved ED, she was finally free.

She fell asleep.

Umber couldn't believe it when he came back. He came closer.

Breathing softly, she was asleep.

He checked her pulse. Nice, regular.

A good vein, right there. An easy shot for a pro.

He grabbed the syringe in his pocket.

He felt eyes, watching him.

He looked around. Nothing.

The syringe.

Eyes, burning him.

His skin crawled.

He stepped out.

Later.

55

George woke up.

Something was wrong.

He sat up listening to the death rattle. He knew it. The sound of his friend choking on his own blood. *Vietnam. I won't forget it till the day I die. Maybe today.*

He saw the old rocking chair with Mary's knitting. *I'm not in Vietnam. Just a nightmare.* He relaxed.

The rattle came back, coarser now. He stood up on shaky legs—that head injury had screwed up his balance. Heart racing, he wobbled to the bedroom. Mary's bedroom.

He turned on the lights.

Mary, leaning over the side of the bed, was throwing up blood.

She's not throwing up. It's spurting out of her like the water out of a cracked hose. Blood dripping down from the mirror, the kids' soccer trophies, Mary's picture of her first communion. Eleven year-old Mary, solemnly dressed in bridal white, now covered by blood splatter like Dracula's bride.

It was a massacre scene like he hadn't yet seen. Not even

in Vietnam. Mary's eyes were pleading for help, but she couldn't speak. Her breath was a blood fountain. His knees gave. He dropped on the bed next to her. He grabbed the phone and dialed 911.

Her blood was spraying him, warm, alive, dying.

He put a pillow behind her to prop her up. He held her hand.

"Dickson, Hunter Street, number 13. Exit 29. Yes, she's alive and breathing. Awake and alert. She's bleeding from her mouth and nose. Yes, both. No, no blood thinners. No, no trauma. She has lung cancer. Yes, I'm holding her up. She can't talk. How long? Ten minutes," he told Mary.

Her eyes were looking into death. Her gaze softened. Her eyes closed. Her rigid body grew heavy.

She was slipping away.

"I love you, baby. I'll take care of you."

Her head dropped on his shoulder. She coughed. A blood clot the size of a child's fist landed in his lap.

The army taught him to deal with bleeding—apply pressure, they said. A single finger if possible. If that doesn't do it, try a tourniquet. Tie it tight enough to stop the bleeding. Release every twenty minutes to allow some oxygen to the tissue downstream. Place it upstream of the bleeding, they said.

That would be around her neck.

He couldn't put a tourniquet there. Pressure wouldn't do it either. Unless he closed her mouth and her nose. She would suffocate.

An eternity later, when the sirens arrived, she was no longer awake.

The EMTs, his old friends Roy and Frank, looked scared. They wanted to stop and put in an IV and start fluids.

George said no. They listened, though they shouldn't have. He was not their boss, but he was an old friend and an ER nurse. They lay her on the stretcher and ran with her.

His old shaky hands got in the IV as they were flying to the hospital with lights and sirens. He drew bloods, most importantly the pink tube, the type and cross for a blood transfusion.

She was still alive when they got there. Barely.

Brenda was waiting in the ambulance bay.

"Who's on?" George asked.

Covered in blood from head to toes, like the killer in a cheap movie, he walked with the stretcher, holding Mary's hand.

"Dr. Umber and Dr. Crump."

"Call Kurt please."

"It's Umber's turn to get the new patient..."

"Call Kurt."

She directed the stretcher to Room 3.

"Dr. Crump to Room 3," the speaker coughed.

Kurt did all he could. He gave her blood and TXA. He called the pulmonary specialist.

"She's bleeding from her lung. The tumor must have eroded into a blood vessel. I can't fix that. They can."

He'd selectively intubated the lung that wasn't bleeding, to give her oxygen while keeping the blood from drowning her, but she wasn't doing well. Her blood pressure dropped. The bleeding restarted.

She bled and bled.

Her heart stopped.

The bleeding stopped too.

"Defibrillator!" Kurt said, his fists tight in his pockets, biting his lower lip to keep from crying.

"Charge the defibrillator."

"Don't," George sobbed. "She deserves better."

"Does she have a DNR form?"

"We talked about it. She knew the end was close. She was OK with it. I wasn't. We never told the kids. They'd have enough time to suffer later."

"You have a power of attorney?"

"Yes."

"I'm sorry, George. Let me know if I can help."

"Thank you."

George sat holding Mary's hand. Her body got cold. She stiffened. He thought about their good days. And the bad. *I wish I was a better husband. How am I going to tell the kids? What will I do?*

When Brenda returned, he had decided. He had done what he could for Mary. Time to deal with the rest.

"Is Dr. Steele here today?"

Brenda gave him an odd look.

"No."

"Tomorrow?"

"No. You haven't heard?'

"Heard what?"

Brenda looked around, making sure nobody could hear. "She was arrested yesterday."

"Arrested? Dr. Steele? Why?"

"She apparently lost her shit and attacked Umber. They said she cut him open. She'd have killed him if the police hadn't intervened. They sedated her and put her in handcuffs."

"Dr. Steele? Are you sure?"

"Yes. Hard to believe, in ten years I've never seen her lose it."

"Why?"

"Something about her daughter. I'm not sure. I wasn't here yesterday; that's just what I heard."

"Thanks, Brenda."

"Sure. I think it's bullshit."

"Yep."

Time to see Zagarian.

56

Emma poured herself a glass of wine. She hadn't eaten since yesterday. She took a sip of the heavy, dry, demanding red, its intense aromas of black currant and vanilla softening its tannins. It was a 2011 Pauillac, a Chateau La Tour L'Aspic.

She had decided to celebrate today. She had opened her most expensive wine. *I could toast myself...but that would be silly.* She toasted the bottle instead, touching her glass to the gray tower on the label, and leaned back to rest her neck.

She watched a rerun of *Chopped*, her favorite show. The appetizer round was over. The fleshy blonde with her breasts spilling out got chopped. *Good. This show isn't about breasts. Unless it's chicken. Or duck.*

She'd tried to reach Zagarian. No luck. After a night at the hospital, she'd spent the morning at the police department.

"Why did you attack Dr. Umber?"

"I didn't. He attacked me."

"Why would he attack you?"

"There's been a slew of overdoses. He's the drug dealer."

"Dr. Umber?"

"Yes. I found two pill bottles in his bag and..."

"What were you doing in his bag?"

"I was looking for proof that he's been selling drugs..."

"Did you find it?"

"I found the pill bottles and..."

"You handled them?"

"Yes."

"How do you think we can use them as proof now?"

Emma shrugged.

"He says you attacked him and almost killed him because he's dating your daughter."

"Yes, but..."

"Dr. Steele, I strongly suggest that you get a lawyer," the detective said.

She had refused a lawyer. She didn't have one.

She'd asked about Zagarian. He wasn't available. She broke down and called Victor. He got her a lawyer whose sharp teeth and unruly white hair made him look like a shark with a Hemingway wig.

The shark got her out on bail, but she had to surrender her passport. She was not to get within half a mile of Umber. The ED was off limits. She took another sip of wine.

My job is over. My career too. What am I going to do? I can cook. Maybe I can work as a chef.

She poured the last of the bottle. Her shoulders had softened. Her pain had dulled. The facts hadn't changed, but her mood had. Good enough.

It feels good to not give a shit!

The doorbell rang. She ignored it. She wasn't in the mood for visitors. It rang again. She broke down and opened the door.

It was Zagarian.

"How are you?"

"Better now," she said, lifting her glass. "You?"

"I'm sorry I wasn't there this morning."

"I'm sorry I was."

"What happened?"

She told him. She told him about Taylor. She told him Umber would let her off the hook if she kept mum about the drugs. She didn't tell him that Taylor was going to sink her to help her lover, nor that life, as she knew it, was over.

"Why did you attack him?"

"I didn't. He attacked me."

"They say you almost killed him."

"Sadly, that's not true."

"That's a silly thing to say. There's no recovery from that. You career would be over."

"It's over already."

He shook his head. "I wish you hadn't done it. I especially wish you hadn't gone through his bag, leaving your prints. Now we have no proof. We don't even have a reason to search his place. No judge would give us a warrant based on the evidence we have. I'll have to speak to your daughter. Will you be there?"

"Nope. Ask her father. She's better behaved around him."

Zagarian nodded.

"I do have some good news though. We found Spider's ex-wife.

Spider's ex-wife?

"Jessy. You know her."

I do?

"You saved her life the other night. The pedestrian hit by a truck in a hit-and-run."

The woman with the spider tattoo! "Did she say anything useful?"

"Maybe. I don't know where you got this oak tree—and I don't want to—but the knife inside it had blood stains. We're working on the DNA. We found the Spider's journal. He knew he was playing a risky game, so he left a trail."

After he left, Emma spent the night wondering whether to go to culinary school or look into becoming a drug rep.

I shouldn't waste all the years I spent in medicine. They cost me my youth and my marriage.

Thanks to Umber, I may start selling drugs too!

57

TAYLOR'S HEADACHE made her sick. *I wish I had some Tylenol. It can't be long now. We've been here for hours.*

She'd held strong, like Dick told her to.

"Admit that we're together—they already know. Deny anything having to do with drugs. You had a headache. I gave you Tylenol. You felt better. That's it. Don't say anything more."

"Of course." His hands made love to her. She moved closer to taste his chest.

"You won't break down under pressure? You won't feel sorry for your mom and sink me?"

"I hate her." She kissed his shoulder, then moved lower. "I'd sink her just for the fun of it."

"I love you."

"I love you."

Taylor smiled, remembering the rest of the night. *It was epic.* Somebody coughed. She snapped back to the present.

Detective Z, the good-looking one with short gray hair, looked at her like she was filth.

He's not that good looking, and he's old.

"What did you do with the pills?"

"I took them. They were Tylenol."

"What about those you gave to your friends?"

"I gave them some Tylenol too, when they had a headache. It made them feel better." *They know I'm lying, but they can't prove it. I'm getting tired. I need a lawyer.* She turned to Victor. "Daddy, can you get me a lawyer?"

Victor shrugged. "I'll try. I'm running out of lawyers here. I gave my last one to your mother."

He'd tried to talk her into helping her mother.

She'd held strong, like Umber had told her, but she'd had enough.

"I want a lawyer."

"Sure," Z. said. "We'll wait for the lawyer. In the meantime, let me introduce you to somebody. She's got some interesting things to tell you."

He pushed a button. The door opened.

Kayla came in, resplendent in her golden high heels and wine-colored leather jacket. She smiled. Taylor smiled back. She knew Kayla. She had been her babysitter. She was cool. Taylor wished she had a mother like that.

Detective Z. pulled out a chair. Kayla sat. "Would you tell Taylor about Dr. Umber?"

"Of course. Taylor, Dick and I, we are in a relationship."

Taylor didn't understand. She replayed that statement in her head. Again. She got it.

That's their bullshit. They want me to spill the beans. They got Kayla to play their dirty game. She always liked Mother. She's lying.

"Really?" She hated Kayla.

"Yes. We got engaged the day before yesterday."

Taylor looked at the ring. Her eyes hurt. Her heart did,

too. It was a gaudy affair, sparkling even in the grimness of the police room.

"I don't believe you."

"You should. I have never lied to you."

"I don't."

"Well, then…" Kayla opened her designer bag and took out a pile of papers. "These are our flight reservations. We're flying to Mexico in two weeks."

She showed them to Taylor, who didn't even glance at them. Kayla shrugged and handed them to Zagarian. She took out her iPhone and came close to Taylor.

I want to hit her. Her heavy sweet perfume makes me sick.

"There're Dick and Eden, ice fishing. There we are having dinner at the Cricket. There we are…"

Taylor didn't need an explanation for that one. It was a selfie; they were lying on a bearskin in front of the fireplace.

She recognized the mounted deer head above the fireplace. It was missing the third point of its right antler. She'd spent a night with Dick in that very room, on that bearskin.

Less than a month ago. That's when I got grounded and lost my phone. Mike called, but I didn't answer. Then Mike died.

"How long has this being going on?" Her throat was so dry that she could hardly swallow. Her heart hurt.

"A few weeks."

"Are you really engaged to him?"

"Yes, I am."

Taylor started crying. She cried for the love that proved to be a hoax. She cried for betraying her mother. More than anything, she cried because her mother had been right. *Again. I hate her. Oh, how I hate her!* She'd never felt so empty, useless, and stupid.

The one person she hated more than she hated her mother was Umber. He'd lied to her, he'd used her, he'd taken advantage of her in every way. She hated him so much, she could hardly breathe.

I'll destroy him. Even if that gets Mother off the hook. Even if it destroys me.

Victor tried to put his arms around her, but she shook him off. She turned to Zagarian.

"I'll tell you whatever you want to know. Just ask."

58

Kayla walked out of the police department smiling. She looked beautiful and serene, but deep inside her heart ached. For the pain she'd inflicted on Taylor. For the hate in Taylor's eyes.

I didn't have a choice. I had to help Emma. And I had to screw Dick. Both.

She had to tell Taylor the truth. It hurt. She had been there only yesterday.

Last night Kurt had rung her doorbell.

She didn't want him there. It was over. She was wearing Dick's ring.

He waited and waited.

She broke down and opened the door.

His eyes were loving and sad.

He's sorry for me.

"I need to speak to you."

"Go ahead."

"Kayla, we need to talk."

Reluctantly, she let him in.

"It's about Umber."

"That subject is over."

"Kayla, he's married."

"I don't believe you."

"He's married. He has two young children. Look!" He took out his cell phone. He started shuffling through pictures. An attractive woman in her thirties. Two kids about Eden's age. They looked like twins. Dick. Lounging near a pool, getting in a minivan, carrying shopping bags into a house. They looked like a happy family.

They couldn't be. That was Dick, her fiancé. He'd just given her a diamond ring.

"This is Mrs. Patricia Umber, with Dodie and Kitty. You know Dick."

"I don't believe you."

"There's her phone number. Call her."

Kayla didn't want to. She looked at the pictures again. *They're a family. Divorced, maybe? He told me that he's been married and has kids. Maybe he's just visiting? I need to know.*

She called. A woman answered.

"The Umber residence."

"May I speak to Dr. Umber?" Kayla asked, swallowing the knot that choked her.

"He's not available right now. Can I help you? I'm his wife, Patricia."

Kayla tried to breathe through the pain. It was suffocating.

"No, thank you. I'll call back."

She hung up. She looked at Kurt. "Are you happy now?"

Kurt looked anything but happy.

"No, Kayla, I'm not happy. Your pain hurts me. I'm here to help a friend. Emma needs your help."

He told her.

She'd had no choice but to break Taylor's heart. She'd done it. *Time to go home and cry.*

59

ZAGARIAN SAID IT CLEARLY, but Emma had trouble believing it.

"I'm off the hook? How come?"

"Thank your friends. George first. When Mary died, he came to see me. He'd been blackmailing Umber. He risked getting indicted in order to help you."

"What did he have on Umber?"

"Umber gave away opiate scripts like candy. He had patients asking for him by name. George thought it was odd, until he saw him accidentally drop a pack of fentanyl powder. Then he understood. He asked for money. It worked. You know what happened when he went back for more."

Emma nodded.

"Then Kurt. He was so mad that he hired a detective to sink Umber. He found out he was married, and he told Kayla, who talked Taylor into telling the truth. Heartbroken, Taylor decided to support you."

"More likely she decided to destroy Umber."

"That's semantics. All in all, you're clear."

"What next?"

"He'll go to jail for drug dealing and attempted murder of George. More if we can prove his role in Ken's death. We're also investigating his possible involvement with the hit-and-run attack on the Spider's ex-wife.

"By the way, the knife in the oak tree has Ken's blood and the Spider's prints. Umber's medical license is history."

"Too bad. He was a good doctor."

"He's a criminal."

"He was still a good doctor."

Zagarian shook his head. "I'll need you to give a written statement."

"Another one?"

"Yep, another one. I'll call."

"OK."

"And maybe we can do dinner."

The half-smile in his eyes reminded her of early spring.

"Maybe we can."

She sat, looking at the TV. She didn't see it. She thought about the people who had come to help her. She thought about Taylor. Taylor had helped her too, not out of love but out of hate. She had forever struggled with her feelings about Taylor.

I've spent years fretting about Taylor. For better or for worse, our relationship will never be the same. She's still my daughter, but she's no longer a child. She'll have to live with the choices she's made. Her future is hers to decide.

She still wished that she had been a better mother, like she wished that she was slimmer or smarter, but had to accept that she wasn't and was never going to be.

Motherhood is not my thing.

60

TAYLOR COULDN'T SLEEP. She was tired and heartbroken. She was out of pills.

She pulled on her jeans; put on her green jacket; and slowly, carefully, opened the door. The gun.

It was locked in the safe. She'd seen it when her father opened the safe the other day as she was hiding, playing hide-and-seek with the girls. She saw the code—it was her mother's birthday. The Walther PPK/S was the same one he'd taught her how to shoot and clean when she was ten. That was one of the special things they did together, just the two of them.

She punched in the code to open the safe. She put the gun in her right pocket, the ammo in her left. Victor's car started at one touch. She took off, leaving the door open. Hands shaking, eyes blurred with tears, she drove to Dick's place.

She rang the doorbell.

Nothing.

She rang again. Dick opened the door wearing red

shorts and a short arm cast. His mangled face was a symphony in blues and greens. His eyes were slits.

"What are you doing here?"

"I missed you. I came to see you."

"At 2 a.m.?"

She pushed past him, her grief choking her. "Is it true?"

"What?"

"About Kayla. Is it true?"

"What about her?"

"That you love her and you're going to marry her."

"Of course not. I love you. Where did you get such a stupid idea?"

"She said so."

He grew darker. He smiled.

"She lied." He came close, putting his good arm around her. "Taylor, I love you. You are tired. Would you like a pill?"

"Yes, please."

She wanted to forget. She wanted to pretend that none of this had happened, that Kayla didn't exist, that he loved her, like he said.

She took the pill. He took one too.

He held her close. She caressed his chest, his back, his groin. He took off her green jacket and her jeans. He laid her on the bed. He kissed her. He made love to her.

Afterward, when she went to the bathroom and found Kayla's perfume, she didn't get upset. She'd known it all along, but she chose to put it out of her mind to enjoy his lovemaking one more time. She showered, dried herself with the snow-white towel, and then sprayed herself with Kayla's perfume all over. Twice between her legs.

He'd fallen asleep. She picked up her jacket off the floor and took out the gun. She loaded it.

His eyes opened, wide. His fear trembled in them like a

cannibal lizard. She lifted the gun with her right arm straight, pointing it between his eyes. Just above the nose.

"Don't," he choked. "Taylor, don't."

"Why not?"

"I love you, Taylor. You know I love you."

"I know you do. I love you too." She aimed at the little scar below his left eyebrow, the one she knew so well. She'd kissed it a thousand times. Her finger turned white as she pressed the trigger. Gently...

"Taylor, don't!" He jumped out of bed as the door crashed open. Emma flew in.

61

"TAYLOR, DON'T," Emma said.

Taylor's eyes didn't move. Her gun followed Umber without fail. The green dot of a laser would have painted his scar.

"Why not?"

"It will destroy your life. You'll go to jail for years! You'll be an old woman by the time you come out."

"My life is already destroyed."

"Not yet. It just feels like it."

"He's destroyed me already. He didn't do you any favors, either. Why not kill him?

"Because you'll get caught! You'll go to jail."

"Not necessarily. Don't move!" she barked, as Umber tried to sneak to the door.

"Sit," she said, pointing with her chin, her arm following him. "We could kill him and hide the body. They'll think he ran away."

"Your father knows you came here with his gun. He called me."

"He won't tell. He doesn't like him either."

"Taylor, please. He'll go to jail, and they'll destroy him there. Please don't do this to yourself."

"I can't. I can't let him go. I need to see him dead."

"Ok, then, let me kill him instead," Emma said.

"You?"

"Why not? I hate him just as much as you do. I'd rather go to jail than see you go."

"How are we gonna get rid of the body?"

"We can't. If we kill him, we'll have to pay."

"OK." Taylor handed her the gun. Dick dashed through the open door.

Outside, Zagarian was waiting. The cuffs clicked.

Emma put the safety on the gun.

"It's over."

Taylor sobbed.

Emma picked up the jacket and helped her into it, then opened her arms.

Taylor sank into them.

"It's over baby."

62

EMMA LOOKED IN THE MIRROR. She'd pulled out all the stops: new haircut, lipstick, foundation, *and* mascara. New white coat.

This is as good as I get.

She'd taken time off after the Umber fiasco. She debated whether to stay or move on. The night in Room 6 haunted her.

They had abandoned her. She had never felt more alone. She'd been heartbroken. She wanted to leave, but her pride had kept her here. She couldn't run away. She had to look them in the eye and see them blush.

Back straight, head held up high, she walked to her desk.

A flower arrangement as big as a Christmas tree.

A banner stretched across the ED. "Welcome back, Dr. Steele! We love you, Emma!"

The steel in her back melted. Hug after hug—Brenda, Kelly, Judy, Alex, and Kurt— were all happy to see her.

It was a homecoming like she'd never hoped for.

But...why? If they care for me, why? Why did they abandon me?

"They didn't want to humiliate you," Sal said. "They respected your dignity. They thought it was more important to you than compassion. If you needed something, you'd let them know."

What I thought was indifference was a sign of respect.
Fuck communication!

63

THE DOORBELL RANG.

Taylor was in no mood for visitors, but they insisted.

Pretty flowers. He's not too shabby, either.

"I'm looking for Dr. Steele."

"She isn't home right now. Can I help you?"

His eyes swept over her, taking in her swollen breasts and slim waist, and then came back to hers. He blushed.

"I want to thank her."

"Come in then."

He sat awkwardly, his flowers on his lap.

"I'm Taylor, her daughter. What did you want to thank her for?"

"I'm Eric. Eric Weiss. She saved my life. My doctors said that I wouldn't be alive, but for her."

"What happened to you?

"I accidentally overdosed."

Taylor nodded.

They talked about the weather, about his work, about her school. He recommended nursing.

They planned for a movie next week.

It shouldn't show yet.

The day she went for her abortion, she had made up her mind.

Then, a young mother holding a tiny infant passed by, glowing like Boticelli's Madonna. She didn't notice Taylor or the people staring at her, not even the proud waiting father. She was absorbed in the scrunched little face of her infant, and the love in her eyes had no end.

Taylor's heart skipped a beat.

She wanted that. She wanted to love like that. She wanted to look at somebody the way this mother looked at her ugly baby.

This love was growing inside her, and she was about to pull it out like a bad tooth.

They wheeled her to the OR. The doctor came in.

"I changed my mind. I don't want an abortion. I want to go home."

They wheeled her back out.

She didn't tell anyone. Not even Umber. It was her secret.

She kept it to herself until that day when Emma didn't shoot Umber.

That day she told her.

64

THE SHADOWS WERE LONG, and the air was crisp as Emma dropped Taylor off. It wasn't close to home, but it was the best rehab for hundreds of miles.

"Mom, I've been thinking. Did you bring the police there that night?

"No. Your father did."

"Did you know they were there?"

"No. But I thought they'd be coming."

"Were you really going to kill him?"

"Sure, why not?"

"But you were going to go to jail!"

"Well, I thought I could really use some rest. I wanted to be a good mother and keep you out of jail. And I wanted to kill him. I still do."

"They'll take care of him in jail."

"Yes."

Taylor nodded. Emma started the engine.

Taylor wasn't showing yet, except for the glow. *Victor was right. She already loves this baby. No matter what.*

"Mom!"

"Yes?"

"I love you, Mom."

Emma didn't cry—she never cried.

"I love you too, baby."

Things were never going to be the same between them.

Emma was never going to be the same.

I may not be the world's best mother, nor the best doctor, but I'm the best I can be.

I'm Dr. Emma Steele, and Taylor's mom. As best I can.

I'm OK.

WHAT IF THE person who's supposed to save your life is actually trying to end it? Find out in **ER CRIMES,** the chilling medical thriller series that will leave you breathless.

AFTERWORD

I hope you liked *OVERDOSE* as much as I loved writing it. If you did, **please take a minute to leave a review** and tell a friend. It will help other readers like you, and I'd really appreciate it.

Go to **RadaJonesMD.com** to sign up for updates and freebies, and to get in touch. I'd love to hear from you.

Rada

ABOUT THE AUTHOR

Rada was born in Transylvania, ten miles from Dracula's Castle. Growing up between communists and vampires taught her that humans are fickle, but you can always trust dogs and books. That's why she read every book she could get, including the phone book (too many characters, not enough action), and adopted every stray she found, from dogs to frogs.

After joining her American husband, she spent years studying medicine and working in the ER and on cruise ships all over the world, but she still speaks like Dracula's cousin.

Rada, her husband Steve, and their dog Guinness live in a cozy Adirondack cabin where they spend their days hiking, reading, and dreaming about traveling to faraway places.

facebook.com/RadaJonesMD

twitter.com/JonesRada

instagram.com/RadaJonesMD

bookbub.com/profile/rada-jones

EXCERPT FROM MERCY

Angel

I love kids.

Pretty kids. Nice kids. Normal kids.

Not this. This is not a kid.

This is thirty pounds of human flesh kept alive by devices. Peg tube, tracheostomy, ventilator. He's got contractures everywhere. He's so folded he'd fit in my carry on. Not that I'd want to take him anywhere.

I check his chart. Evan. He's twelve. He can't see, he can't talk, he can't eat, he can't breathe.

What's the point of being alive? If you call this alive. He doesn't know he's alive. He can't think.

Can he feel? Let's find out.

I stick a #18 needle in his heel.

He pulls away and tries to scream. He can't. He snorts.

He feels pain. That sucks. I wouldn't have my dog live like this! Any dog! And he's human, if only in name.

I look around. They're all busy.

I turn off the alarms and I detach his tracheostomy from the

*vent. I cover it with my palm, pretending I'm cleaning it. I wait
for the heart to stop.*

It takes forever.

I reconnect the vent and leave.

Bye-bye, Evan. If they ask, tell them Carlos sent you!

~

MERCY

Printed in Great Britain
by Amazon